W9-AVW-909

"Are you trying to get yourself killed?"

A strong hand clasped my shoulder and spun me face-to-face with my favorite local law enforcer. Serras's dark gaze came down hard on the bruised line of flesh across my throat. He shook me a little as he muttered a curse.

Before I could answer, that mouth came down on mine. The kiss was as hard as the man, without a touch of tenderness that would have had me pushing him away and sorely disappointed.

We indulged ourselves for thirty seconds, maybe a minute, his hands fisting into the length of my hair and my body meeting his, sensation for sensation. When it was over, I released him as suddenly as he'd grabbed me. I took a ragged, dissatisfied breath, knowing I would yearn for more for a long time....

Dear Harlequin Intrigue Reader,

You won't be able to resist a single one of our May books. We have a lineup so shiver inducing that you may forget summer's almost here!

- *Executive Bodyguard* is the second book in Debra Webb's exciting new trilogy, THE ENFORCERS. For the thrilling conclusion, be sure you pick up *Man of Her Dreams* in June.

- Amanda Stevens concludes her MATCHMAKERS UNDERGROUND series with *Matters of Seduction*. And the Montana McCalls are back, in B.J. Daniels's *Ambushed!*

- We also have two special premiers for you. Kathleen Long debuts in Harlequin Intrigue with *Silent Warning*, a chilling thriller. And LIPSTICK LTD., our special promotion featuring sexy, sassy sleuths, kicks off with Darlene Scalera's *Straight Silver*.

- A few of your favorite Harlequin Intrigue authors have some special books you'll love. Rita Herron's *A Breath Away* is available this month from HQN Books. And, in June, Joanna Wayne's *The Gentlemen's Club* is being published by Signature Spotlight.

Harlequin Intrigue brings you the best in breathtaking romantic suspense with six fabulous books to enjoy. Please write to us—we love to hear from our readers.

Sincerely,

Denise O'Sullivan
Senior Editor
Harlequin Intrigue

Darlene Scalera

Straight SILVER

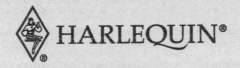

HARLEQUIN®

TORONTO • NEW YORK • LONDON
AMSTERDAM • PARIS • SYDNEY • HAMBURG
STOCKHOLM • ATHENS • TOKYO • MILAN • MADRID
PRAGUE • WARSAW • BUDAPEST • AUCKLAND

If you purchased this book without a cover you should be aware
that this book is stolen property. It was reported as "unsold and
destroyed" to the publisher, and neither the author nor the
publisher has received any payment for this "stripped book."

Thanks to all, much too numerous to name,
that have taken me here to this tenth book.
With gratitude.

ISBN 0-373-88622-5

STRAIGHT SILVER

Copyright © 2005 by Darlene Scalera

All rights reserved. Except for use in any review, the reproduction or
utilization of this work in whole or in part in any form by any electronic,
mechanical or other means, now known or hereafter invented, including
xerography, photocopying and recording, or in any information storage
or retrieval system, is forbidden without the written permission of the
publisher, Harlequin Enterprises Limited, 225 Duncan Mill Road,
Don Mills, Ontario, Canada M3B 3K9.

All characters in this book have no existence outside the imagination of
the author and have no relation whatsoever to anyone bearing the same
name or names. They are not even distantly inspired by any individual
known or unknown to the author, and all incidents are pure invention.

This edition published by arrangement with Harlequin Books S.A.

® and TM are trademarks of the publisher. Trademarks indicated with
® are registered in the United States Patent and Trademark Office, the
Canadian Trade Marks Office and in other countries.

www.eHarlequin.com

Printed in U.S.A.

ABOUT THE AUTHOR

A native New Yorker, Darlene graduated magna cum laude from Syracuse University with a degree in public communications. She worked in a variety of fields, including telecommunications and public relations, before devoting herself full-time to fiction writing.

A charter member of the Saratoga Chapter of Romance Writers of America, she served on its board for five years. She is also a member of the Capital Region Chapter of Romance Writers of America. She has presented writing workshops at national and regional writers' conferences as well as at local universities and colleges.

She lives happily ever after in upstate New York with her husband, Jim, and their two teenage children, J.J. and Ariana. Visit her at www.darlenescalera.com.

CAST OF CHARACTERS

Silver LeGrande—Born with a stripper's name and a brick-house bod to fulfill her certain destiny, she's left the daily bump and grind to go community college coed. But when someone strangles her former colleague, and no one seems to care, Silver turns from the classroom to the only cop she knows who will give a damn.

Detective Alexi Serras—The last thing he needed was a partner. Especially a five-foot-eleven ex-stripper with a yard of crayon-red hair and attitude to match her assets.

Billie West—Owner of Memphis's most infamous nightclub, Billie ran a clean joint, keeping the customers and the cops happy. Silver had been her top draw, and Billie had suspected it was only a matter of time before she came back to the club. But neither had imagined the reason would be murder.

Della Devine—By the time she was murdered, she was working the poles in a sleazy operation on the lower side.

Paul Chumsky—Resident pro at a country club for Memphis moneybags, Chumsky had a charm that kept him in the good graces of the club's male members and in the firm beds of their wives. But the evening before she died he'd spent with Della Devine.

Chapter One

I should have known better. No one gets away scot-free. Certainly not ex-exotic dancers. Not even ones with fifteen and a half community college credits and a legitimate chauffeur's license. Auntie always said it had taken four generations of LeGrande women to produce another as tough as my Great-Great-Grandma Bettina "Brass Buttons" Mae. Four generations plus a thick-lipped midway worker from Quebec blind in the right eye, my momma's weak knees for a foreign accent her legendary downfall. But as the officer pulled back the sheet on Della Devine, I feared not even the blood of four generations of LeGrande women and a one-eyed Canadian carny would save me this time.

Not that I hadn't seen death. Before my breasts fully developed and my age advanced to legal level, I'd cashiered part-time at the Piggly Wiggly, and I was working on the morning

Florence Sutton went in to use the public toilet and never came out. After a period of some patience, her acquaintance, Loris Martin, who the meaner folks in town liked to speculate was Flo's unnatural lover, alerted the day manager. Fire trucks, police cruiser, ambulance came lights whirling, sirens wailing into the lot. The door was broken down, and there was Flo, dead as the Christmas hog come smoking season. Wilson Bintliff, Tipton County's most eligible undertaker heard the call over his scanner and arrived in a less flashy but equally timely manner only to stand around with everyone else, tapping his polished Florsheims to the tune of "She'll Be Coming around the Mountain." Not much else could be done until the body was pronounced, but seeing it was now lunch hour, which Doc Flaherty and his fleshy nurse, Suzie Toomis, always spent with the answering machine on and their pants off, it was going to be a wait.

The rest room was yellow-taped off but if you snuck in behind the bakery counter and cranked your neck, you could get an eyeful of poor Flo. The more irreverent of us took a peek. Even in death Flo had a way of looking at you as if she'd smelled the silent fart you'd let at last Sunday's service. Stood to reason the same people who whispered about Flo's sexual partialities would add this comeuppance was well deserved, but I'd imagined a person had to do a lot more than flare her nostrils extrawide to deserve to pass away with her pantyhose around her knees in the public rest room of the Piggly Wiggly.

I looked down. Della stared straight up at me but saw nothing. *Oh girl, what'd you do to deserve this?*

"Cleaning lady found her next to the dumpster behind the club where she was working."

"Billie's?"

"No, the Oyster Club."

I raised my gaze to Detective Alexi Serras. The Greek genes in his hard-boned face gave him an edge to stare strongly at any woman and get away with it. Except me. Corpses and cops made me cranky.

"Cleaning woman didn't recognize her, but–" Serras lifted the middle of the sheet. "The tattoo jogged her memory."

I looked at the rose-vined double D high on the buttock. Billie herself had had strict policies on body art and piercing along with other excesses of "tastefulness." She'd approved Della's choice, although made it well-known that in her opinion tattoos were for sailors and convicts.

"Cleaning woman remembered one of the day girls talking about a new girl at the club, working prime time. Della Devine. You were listed as the emergency contact in her employee file."

Classic case of the blind leading the blind.

"It's Della."

He reached to draw the sheet over her face. I grabbed his wrist. Serras shot me a look that could have curdled cream. I held on. Great-Great-Grandma LeGrande would have been proud.

"Give me a moment, will ya."

His expression went bland as if to say, "It's your dime." I let go of his wrist.

"She was working at the Oyster?" I asked. When I'd hung up my boa, Della had still been at Billie's.

"For about three months, according to records at the club. When's the last time you'd seen her?"

"Eight, nine months ago." As an emergency contact, I stunk.

"How long did you know Ms. Devine?"

He said her name as if it'd been hers since birth. I'd noticed he had uttered my name, too, without the usual smirking skepticism, although in my case he would have been correct.

Baptized Silver LeGrande, I was born with a stripper's name and a body that past puberty clinched my destiny.

"About four years." I'd been working the circuit seven years when I came to Billie's. I'd developed a respectable following and feature status. Della had just been promoted from the floor to the poles. As soon as I'd heard the young girl's tag, I'd known we'd get along fine. Baptismal advantage aside, I liked gals with the brass to call themselves Della Devine.

"We both worked at Billie's." The Oyster wasn't as bad as some joints, but in the hierarchy of strip clubs, it wasn't even close to Billie's. Seems like Della had been working her way down the ladder. I looked at her still body. Looked like she'd gotten there.

"You know why she left Billie's?" Serras asked.

A greenish tint above Della's eye spoke of an old bruise. The new bruises along her collarbones said she'd struggled. The purple horizontal stripe across her throat said she'd lost.

"No."

"You're no longer employed at Billie's, either?"

I'd left the daily bump and grind about a year ago and gone collegiate. Maybe that's why

Della had decided I could shimmy to an SOS with the best of them. She'd been wrong.

"Career change."

Not even Della's two-pack-a-day habit had etched any fine lines in her face yet. The skin was as smooth as a newborn's butt with only a slight bluish undercast.

I leaned forward, drawn by a mark on Della's throat more defined than the other signs of struggle.

"You're no longer in the entertainment industry?"

"I go to community college." Let Serras stick that in his Krispy Kreme. I moved in closer, outlining the mark without touching it. Force had branded the shape of a double *D* into the tender flesh of Della's throat.

"You see this?"

"Double *D*," Serras confirmed. "Bartender at the Oyster Club said she had this gold piece she used to slip on her G-string?"

"A gold double *D*. Kind of like a signature." I straightened, looked Serras in the eyes. "Called it her lucky charm."

Serras was clever enough not to raise an eyebrow.

"Did she have any unusual sexual practices?" He was referring to the horizontal line across

Della's throat. Cut off the oxygen at the moment of climax and achieve the ultimate orgasm. Unless something or someone went wrong. Then it became a matter of finding a plausible explanation for the well-wishers at the wake.

"Scarfing wasn't her style."

"You sure?"

I wasn't sure of anything at this point.

"Maybe it was someone else's?" Serras ventured.

I narrowed my gaze. "That how you guys are going to write this off?"

Serras's pupils dilated. He was getting interested now. He said nothing.

"This was more than a night of sexual fun and games gone awry." I had just finished my second semester of English comp.

He looked at Della on her steel bed.

I waited until he lifted his gaze. I met the black in his eyes. "She was murdered."

He played it cop cool. "There'll be an autopsy."

Way too much information before lunch.

"What about her family? She have anyone in the area?"

"Her younger brother was in the service. Last I knew he was stationed right near here at Fort

Grant. She once mentioned a grandmother in Pittsburgh raised her. Never said what happened to her real parents."

"She didn't mention anyone else?"

I looked at Della's pale lips. Most gals were only too happy to give you a blow-by-blow of how they'd been done wrong or hung out to dry—more times than not by their own flesh and blood, but not Della. She didn't confide much, but she didn't bitch, either. Grousing was not her style. She had dignity. If Jackie O had been a stripper, she would have been Della Divine.

"No." I answered Serras.

"What about boyfriends?"

"Sure."

"Anybody special?"

"Strippers don't usually go steady."

"How 'bout friends, enemies? Anyone stand out?"

I shook my head. I'd never have a career as an emergency contact.

"Ms. Devine have any problems with any of the other girls at Billie's?"

I shook my head again, returning my gaze to the corpse. I remembered a bright blonde with fake breasts, a whole lotta leg and a corn-pone wholesomeness not usually associated with someone from Pittsburgh. Her specialty had been tassels. I felt lousy.

"What was her real name?" I asked Serras.

"Doris Mickel."

I reached for the sheet and drew it up over her face.

Serras smoothed a wrinkle in the sheet, then slid Della/Doris back before stepping away from her. If he'd been the pencil-pushing type bucking for Administration, I'd have written the gesture off as anal. But it being not even noon yet and already too long a day, I decided to allow myself the delusion this cop might really care what happened to a twenty-seven-year-old stripper with a violet choker and green bruises for eye shadow.

"Got any other thoughts on what happened to her?" I wasn't deluded enough to think he'd start spouting out theories, but my motto is "You Can't Fault a Girl for Trying."

"We'll be investigating all possibilities." He gestured for me to precede him out of the morgue.

I didn't move. "Maybe someone was trying to rob the Oyster and Della got in the way?"

"How 'bout a cup of coffee, Ms. LeGrande?"

It was July in Memphis. Just breathing made you sweat. Officer Serras wanted more than to extend hospitality. I glanced at my Rolex knockoff. I was taking a few summer courses at the college, catching up on credits. "I've got Principles of Macroeconomics in ten minutes."

Serras didn't crack a smile. Della could have done worse for a homicide detective.

"Was she killed in the club, then dumped out back?" I probed.

This time Serras took my elbow, steering me toward the door.

"We'll investigate all angles."

"The bruises on her body, the pooling of blood suggest she was moved from the original crime scene."

Serras glanced at me. I was bluffing, and he knew it, but it was a good bluff, and I sensed he liked my style.

"There'll be a preliminary report filed later today. You can give me a call."

I took his card. "Thanks." I meant it.

"If you remember anything, think of something that might help us learn who did this to Ms. Devine, you can get in touch with me at that number or leave a message. I'll get back to you."

He had used Della's stage name as if he knew it'd please her. And me. He was right.

He led me up one floor. At the public entrance door, he tapped the card still in my hand.

"If you remember anything—"

I nodded. I knew the routine. You don't strip for eleven years without participating in a few police procedures. This was the first time it was this personal, though.

I stopped on the way out to hold the door for a young woman coming up the sidewalk pushing a stroller. Serras was heading toward the back of the station house. As a stripper, I'd become a student of the body but I wasn't even using that excuse this time. I watched him for the pure pleasure. His glutes tightened. His backside became even firmer. Finer. I didn't know if his cop radar sensed I was watching him or he just wasn't taking any chances. I did know one thing though. It wouldn't be the last time I'd see those prime-time buns flex. Like gals called Silver LeGrande and Della Devine, some fates are unavoidable.

Chapter Two

Three miles from campus I pulled a 180 and headed into the heart of the city. Billie's held center stage in a renovated warehouse two short blocks from Beale Street. Only a small sign near the double doors advertised Adult Entertainment. The club's owner, Billie West, ran a clean joint. Topless only, no lap dances, no drugs, and Billie never missed a contribution to the Policemen's Benevolent Association. I parked, went in through the back employees' entrance. The club wouldn't be open for hours, but Billie did her paperwork in the afternoon. She didn't look surprised when I came to the office door. Billie had always expected it was only a matter of time before I'd be back.

"Silver." She welcomed me in her rich contralto as she enfolded me in the reassurance of two hundred pounds plus. She rocked me a little and was kind enough to let me hang on tight.

Billie was a mulatto from New Orleans with golden marcel waves and a variety of lovers. Her mama had sewn the costumes for many of the burlesque stars of Bourbon Street while Billie had listened to the triumphs of "Lottie the Body" and "Tajmah the Jewel of the Nile" and other stories of the glamorous life in the French Quarter clubs. When still on the sweet side of thirty, Billie had convinced one of her boyfriends, an ex-racketeer, to invest in her dream, and Billie's was born—a nightclub in the forties' French Quarter style. Billie's featured an emcee, comics and singers, but it was the girls that brought in the customers.

"So, you finally ready to come back to work? I can start you on the floor, strolling and getting drinks." Billie smiled, showing a gold cap.

I cocked a hip. "When did I ever wait tables?"

"That's only 'cause you never could learn to take orders." Billie's smile split wider, adding another lush fold to her chin. Billie had caught my show one night in an upstart club in Jackson. I'm five-eleven with a yard of crayon-red hair and miraculously not one freckle plus big breasts that even unsupported still look happy. She promised me one-third more than my current nightly take. By the time we finished, she'd guaranteed double my salary and headliner status. I have the attitude to match my assets. The next night I was on her stage.

"You hear about Della?" It was a rhetorical question. Billie had probably known about the murder before I'd even gotten down to the morgue. Part of being a successful club owner was keeping the cops happy...and vice versa.

The dance in her eyes disappeared. "Bit of bad business, this with Della."

She reached for a candy from an inlaid bowl on her desk. She pushed the bowl toward me. I shook my head. Normally I ate like a linebacker, but a dead body did wonders to suppress the appetite.

"I didn't know she'd left the club. You have to let her go?" Della had been known to dabble—coke, crystal meth mostly, but besides a four-day toot when the rest of us girls covered for her, she'd kept her act together and her vices limited to off-club hours. Still, little went on in the club that Billie didn't know about and would only tolerate to a point.

The huge gold hoops in Billie's ears jangled as she nodded. "She'd been on a bender since her brother's death—"

"Her brother's death?" My breath seemed to go. I sank back into the chair.

Billie reached for another candy, unwrapped

the foil slowly and slipped it between her lips. "Ugly incident. Not far from where the child was stationed." Billie sucked on the candy.

"What happened?"

"Seems he was out with the boys, whooping it up. You know G.I.s, give 'em a weekend pass and they think they've got a one-way ticket to Sodom-and-Gomorrah land. When the others decided to call it a night, the boy, Della's brother, either hadn't had enough yet or maybe he just got separated from the others. When he was ready to go home, he must have decided to walk back to the base. He either got lost, stumbled and fell or passed out on the train tracks. By the time the conductor saw him, it was too late."

"He was run over by a train? Lord." The breath left my body again.

"I turned a blind eye to Della's behavior the first couple months, but when things began to get worse instead of better, I realized I wasn't doing the child no favors. I gave her a choice. Get herself into a program and clean herself up or I'd have to let her go. She left. Ended up at the Oyster." Billie's nostrils flared wide. I thought of Flo.

"It was the last time I saw her." Billie tapped an inch-long acrylic fingernail with a crystal in its center on the candy dish's edge.

"Until today I hadn't seen her since I'd left the club. She had me listed as an emergency contact at the Oyster. Makes a little more sense now that I know about her brother."

"Doesn't surprise me. She always did look up to you. After I confronted her about her drug use, she felt the girls here had betrayed her. You know a junkie." Billie's fingernails skimmed the air. "They've always got someone else to blame for their own messes."

"I had to go down this morning, identify the body. A Detective Serras called me."

Billie brought her hands together, steepled her fingers. "Ahh, Lexi."

"You know him?"

Billie gave me a tolerant look. "Father was an officer, too. Killed during a robbery attempt. In his own home."

"His own home?" I echoed.

Billie waited to see if I was finished interrupting. "Royce had just made sergeant then, took the boy under his wing."

Royce was Royce Ealy, now chief of police with, according to the newspapers, an eye toward running for police commissioner next fall.

"What kind of a cop is he?"

"Some say if it wasn't for Royce, Serras would have been busted back to flatfoot years ago."

"Truth or jealousy?"

"Little bit of both. He's got a reputation as a wild card. Hasn't learned to play by the rules yet."

I myself was a work in progress along those lines. Serras and I would have no problems in that area.

"Got busted early on for excessive force. Charges didn't stick. But be careful, *chère,* he's a dangerous man. Not hard to look at." Billie smiled slim, sly. "You look, *chère?*"

"I looked."

Billie released a luxuriant laugh. "You're still one of my girls, you know that, darlin'?" Billie's smile disappeared into sadness. "Della was, too. Despite everything. One of my girls ends up like this. I don't like it."

"What do you think happened?"

Her eyes on me, Billie reached for another candy. "Drugs, the Oyster Club…"

"She was strangled with her own G-string."

Billie sucked silently, for the second time showing no surprise. With her pipeline to the police, she probably knew more details about the murder than I did.

"Kind of an eloquent statement." My English comp acted up again.

"Or a practical one if the killer needed a

weapon." If Billie did know anything about the murder, she wasn't telling.

The phone rang. I stood. Billie motioned me to sit as she glanced at the number on the caller ID screen. "The machine can get it."

I stayed standing. I only had one question left—who killed Della Divine? Billie either didn't have the answer, or if she did she wasn't sharing.

"I've got to go, Billie."

She leaned her impressive bulk back against her chair and nodded as if she understood, just like the first time I'd told her I had to go. She got up to walk me out.

"How's school? Getting straight A's?"

"I'm getting by." I wasn't ready to admit that a dyslexic going to college is equal to a stripper wearing her thong backward onstage—fully exposed and no idea what the hell you're doing.

"Good girl. You do my taxes after you become legit?"

"If you give me the real set of books."

Her laughter became richer. "Still one of my girls, Silver."

She made my name sound like a symphony.

We embraced at the back door. "You hear anything about this thing with Della, you give me a call?" I asked her.

Billie put her hands on my shoulders as if to steady me. "Sometimes, *chère,* a thing like this happens. And there's nothing you or I could have done to stop it."

I left, my body still warm from Billie's embrace, the faint sweet smell of her breath in my nostrils. And an unsettling sensation that she had just lied to me.

I WAS CHECKING the temperature of the chocolate when Adrienne came in. If the chocolate was too cold, you got splinters. Too warm and you got mush. I drew my knife across the square's surface. With a satisfaction like a long sigh, I watched the chocolate curl. Adrienne eyed the orange chiffon cheesecake. "What's wrong?"

I used to drink when I worried. Now I bake. Adrienne scooped a dollop of whipped cream from the mixer bowl and sucked it off her finger while I told her about Della's death. She pulled her finger slowly out of her mouth when I finished. Her lips stayed set in an *O.* Adrienne is a university student and the daughter of my divorced dentist, Herb Bloomberg. Last year Momma had finally made good on her threat to sell Great-Great-Grandma LeGrande's gorilla of a house and head to Biscayne Bay, and for the first time, I got sentimental. I'd worked the circuit for eleven years, eleven very profitable years, but the town of Snake Fish twenty-two miles south of Memphis was home. Sentimentality isn't cheap. Adrienne rents the finished basement. I get a little extra cash to keep this hulk of a house and my childhood illusions alive plus twice-annual free dental cleanings and checkups. Adrienne hasn't had to buy herself a drink in a bar since she moved in with an ex-stripper. We were a match made for the Memphis suburbs.

I placed chocolate curls around the cake's top with a finesse I don't usually possess. Adrienne was seeking comfort from a beater off the mixer when the back door slammed. Great-Aunt Peggilee came in from her pool aerobics class at the Jewish senior center, singing Frankie Laine. She was either still in the throes of exercise endorphins or Charley Diamond had worn his Speedo again.

She eyed the orange chiffon cheesecake. "What's wrong?"

Auntie came with the house. She teases her hair so high it could be a way station for migrating geese. She also favors heavy eyeliner, clip-on earrings, male crooners and fake fur…in Memphis. If Barbie needed a great-aunt, Auntie Peggilee would have been the prototype.

"One of the girls Silver used to work with is in a bad way." Adrienne extended the other beater to my great-aunt. The mutual adoration between Adrienne and her I could only credit to their complete antithesis of each other.

"Pregnant?" Auntie's eyes narrowed, slid to my waist while her tongue flicked at a blob of cream.

"Dead."

We weren't a subtle household.

Auntie licked the beater. Her slitted gaze on me didn't say, "That could have been you." Her eyes with their turquoise lids had seen enough to know it could have been any one of us instead of Della laid out on cold steel this morning.

"That for after the funeral?" Auntie nodded toward the cake. Practicality was Aunt Peggilee's way of coping.

"I guess it could be," I answered, not realizing it until now.

"When is it?"

"I don't know. The police are looking for family. Della had a younger brother in the military, but he was killed in a train accident a few months ago."

"Train accident?"

"He was on the tracks after a heavy night on the town. Not far from the base. They think he was walking home and either fell and knocked himself out or plum passed out. They couldn't stop the train in time." I handed them each a chocolate curl.

"And now the sister is dead?"

Auntie shaved her eyebrows and painted on new ones. They headed beehive level. Auntie doesn't believe in coincidence.

"Strangled." Adrienne supplied, moving on to a spatula.

"Della never really mentioned anybody but her brother, and a grandmother who raised them in Pittsburgh. I suppose if they don't find anybody, the girls at Billie's will take up a collection. Bintliff should give us a fair price."

"You want me to go with you to the service?"

"I don't see any reason."

"Neither do I." Aunt Peggilee put the licked-clean beater in the bowl soaking in the sink, took a swig of her sport drink. "But I will."

I adored my great-aunt Peggilee, too.

I CHECKED IN with Luxury Limousines after my class in fundamentals of info processing, but midweek was always slow. Any jobs that came in went to the old-timers. They didn't need me until the weekend. Adrienne was at her summer job at the university science library where she spent most of her time scouting out premeds. Auntie would be leaving for salsa class followed by Margarita Mania at the Elks. I headed into Memphis, going against the tide of rush-hour traffic. The Oyster Club was in a corner of the city that made respectable folks shake their heads, and campaigning politicians favor for catchy photo ops. But an upward transformation had begun, thanks to a new condominium complex three streets over, whose towers could be seen from the T-shirt stalls on the corner. Come in from the east, and you'd pass a freestanding zone of new construction that took up almost the whole street. The centerpiece was the residential towers that included a health club and underground parking. Enter from the west and you'd see the transvestite hookers, the homeless waiting for St. Francis' shelter to open for lunch, and the exotic dancer marquees, the largest of which was the Oyster Club.

The club was quiet. Peak patron time was hours from now. A thin-haired man sat at the bar, stirring his drink with his pinkie, more interested in the clear liquid than the women dancing on the catwalk. A woman in her cruel forties slapped a cardboard coaster down as I slid onto a stool.

"Ginger ale." Elixir of the reformed.

She brought the drink, cast me a resigned look and waited. Thirty-one-year-old community college coeds, even ex-strippers, don't stop in at Club Oyster at the end of the day for a soft drink.

"I was a friend of Della Devine's." I held out my hand. "Silver LeGrande."

A flash of recognition sparked in her pale eyes. She took my hand, didn't give me her name, but she left my money on the bar. "I heard you left Billie." Her gaze took me in and spit me out. "You looking for a gig here?"

I shook my head. "I'm going to college."

She nodded, no expression. Enough years behind a bar and you heard it all. She wiped the counter. "Sorry about your friend."

"Were you here this morning?"

Her eyes lifted to mine. "My shift doesn't start until noon. As it was, by the time the cops got done scouring this place, we didn't open until four." She looked around. "Not that it matters. Something like this scares people. Business will be off for a while."

"Police said the cleaning woman found her."

"Cindy."

A calico cat jumped on the bar. I started. The bartender backhanded the cat off the counter with a surprisingly elegant swat.

"Damn stray. Throw it out every night, but the girls keep feeding it, leaving it milk." The bartender moved away and, with a similar grace, grabbed a bottle, poured another several clear inches into the empty glass of the man at the bar with the pinkie swizzle stick.

"Cindy works mornings. She doesn't know many of the girls," the woman said as she came back to me. "Couldn't reach the manager. Called 911.

"Police said the woman saw the tattoo. Made her remember Della's name."

"Della Devine." The woman smiled, her bridge work not bad. "I liked that name."

I smiled back. "Me, too."

"Police had Cindy find her file to see if there was family, friend, somebody to contact." The woman paused. "Silver LeGrande," she pronounced with the same surprising elegance she'd used to backhand the cat off the counter.

I sipped my ginger ale. "Did you know Della?"

"I knew her, but I usually work the early shift. She danced second shift. Better money."

"How 'bout the other girls?"

The woman shrugged. "Sure, the late-night girls knew her. They'll be coming in all shook up for a while, sipping something strong between sets. The ones that called in to see if we were open tonight said she was a good kid."

"I heard she had her problems."

The woman's second shrug said, "Don't we all?'

"Some of the girls will be here in a couple hours. They might be able to tell you more." I couldn't fault the woman for clamming up. Self-preservation comes before sympathy.

"What about them?" I looked at the girls working the poles. "They know Della?"

"Lucy worked with her." The bartender tipped her head toward a blonde, her breasts disproportionate to narrow hips and fireplace-poker legs. "The other girl hasn't been here that long."

"Anybody else called? Been by? Family maybe?"

"You and the cops. That's it."

I finished my ginger ale and felt forlorn even with bubbles up my nose.

"Get you something else?"

I snapped the rubber band against my wrist. Two years ago I'd been on the cusp of being a drunk. Some people twelve-stepped their way out. I'd snapped myself sober. Today the skin above my pulse was a mean black and blue.

"Thought I'd wait around, maybe talk to Lucy when she goes on break."

"I'll send her over." The woman walked away.

"The girls have lockers? Some place to store their stuff in the dressing room?"

The woman turned back to me. "There's a few lockers. Not enough for everyone on the busy nights. The girls share."

"Mind if I take a look?"

"Don't know that you'll find much, but go ahead. Police have already been in there, but that don't mean squat. Strung-out stripper strangled with her own G-string. The boys downtown have probably already chalked it up to karma."

She was probably right. I doubted even Officer Serras with his sheet-smoothing hands would lose any sleep tonight over Della Divine.

The back room smelled of smoke and hairspray. Three wooden tables with large rectangle mirrors were covered with makeup bottles, hairspray cans, brushes. A stained couch occupied one corner. The coffee table in front of it was littered with overflowing ashtrays. The lockers were a line of five, industrial brown and scratched. The first held an oversize man's shirt, a black bowtie and a cowboy hat. Two whips and a dog collar hung in the second one. It was a stroll down memory lane. I didn't even know what I was looking for. If there had been any clues, some cop in the crime lab was earning his daily wage going over them now. I opened the third locker, peered inside. It felt better than doing nothing. On a hook hung a long red wig.

"Jane said you wanted to see me."

I jumped, hit my head on the door edge, and swore like a sailor. A girl slumped into a seedy-looking chair in the corner, lit a cigarette, exhaled. She crossed her bony legs, her foot swinging. She'd seen me jump like a scared rabbit. She was one up on me, and she knew it.

"Silver LeGrande." Emergency contact.

"Lucy." She didn't give a last name. "Jane says you knew Della?"

"We worked together at Billie's."

"You dance at Billie's?"

"Used to."

"Where do you dance now?"

"I don't. I'm going to school."

"What for?"

"I want to be an accountant."

The girl studied me with a half-lidded gaze.

Her robe was loose, adding an untidy air about her. She was much younger up close than on the stage. She inhaled, exhaled, didn't offer up anything.

"How well did you know Della?" I asked her.

"We weren't bosom buddies." The words were tough. So was the girl's face. Caring cost you in a club.

"You work the second shift?"

"Usually. I'm pulling a double tonight, filling in for one of the regular girls who got spooked by the whole deal."

"What happened didn't scare you?"

"I got three kids to feed." The girl inhaled hard. "The show goes on." She tapped an ash, ground it into the worn carpet with her foot.

"I heard she was pretty broken up about her brother's death."

"First I heard about it."

"He was run over by a train few months back. Over near Fort Grant where he was stationed."

The girl dragged on her cigarette until the end burned hot orange.

"Something like that, well, it could make a person…" I waited for Lucy to fill in the blanks. She didn't. I tried to make it easy for her. "She was using when I knew her."

The girl shrugged. "I'd seen worse."

So had I. "You know why she came here?"

"The ambiance." The girl gave a tight smile, proud of herself.

"Anybody she was seeing?"

The girl stood and went to the washroom.

"Maybe somebody special?"

"Yeah, they line up at the door here to sweep us off our feet." I heard a small hiss as she pitched her cigarette into the toilet.

"How about any of the customers? Maybe one of the regulars? Someone who likes to get rough?"

Lucy came back into the room, plopped herself down at a dressing table, started applying blush with force. She caught my gaze in the mirror. "I already answered all these questions earlier for the police. What are you looking for anyway?"

I told her the truth. "I don't know."

I had surprised her this time. She smiled. For a moment she was just a young girl enjoying a grin. She reached for a hairbrush. "We worked together, that's pretty much it. She was pretty tight-lipped, didn't go around giving you her life story like there was some fat chance you'd be interested."

"How about the other girls? Anyone she hung out with outside of work?"

"This is a strip club. Not a sorority house." Lucy got up, went over to the lockers. "Listen, I wish I had something to give ya, but I don't. There's a lot of freaks out there. It happens every day."

She opened a locker door, took out a fresh pack of cigarettes.

"So last night just happened to be Della's turn?"

The girl glanced at me over her shoulder. No one had thought of me as naive for a long time...until now. "You got a better explanation?"

"Not yet."

The girl gave a crooked smile, slammed the locker door. "I gotta get to work." She opened the fresh pack of cigarettes, tapped one out and lit it. She didn't move.

"Della was always bumming cigarettes off everybody at Billie's. She do that to you?"

The girl went to the couch, sat on its edge. She crossed her legs and eyed me through the smoke. "Yeah, she was a pain like that."

"She was always trying to quit." I went on, hoping I'd hit a nerve. "Thought if she didn't buy 'em, she wouldn't smoke 'em." Della flashed too real in my memory.

"Yeah, she did that here, too. Never helped

her none. Don't matter much now, anyway, does it?"

I couldn't hold my gaze anymore on the girl with the swinging foot and the slack robe. I turned to leave.

"She used to let a lot of the girls borrow money though. She do that at Billie's?"

I stopped, nodded.

"She'd never harass them about paying her back. She was good like that." The girl tapped the ash off her cigarette and looked at me. "It was as if she didn't care about the money."

"You know anything she did care about?"

Lucy leaned forward and set the cigarette in the ashtray. She picked up a cosmetic bag, took out a lip pencil. "She was meeting someone last night. After her shift." She lined her lips as she talked.

"You know who?"

She smacked her lips together twice. I snapped my rubber band.

"I don't know. I wasn't eavesdropping or anything like that. I came into the dressing room and heard her talking on the phone. Whoever it was, she was telling them she'd meet them after work."

I schooled my features, concealing any excitement. Lucy could be playing me, after all. Some girls have a natural mean streak.

"Did you tell this to the police?"

"I'm telling you."

"Why?"

"You go to college. You're a smart woman." Lucy picked up her cigarette. She took a long draw, stubbed it out and stood.

I found a pen, ripped a blank page out of my pocket planner which was easy since all the pages were blank. I scribbled numbers down. "This is my cell, this is my house." I heard the hope in my voice and didn't even care. I held out the paper to Lucy. "Just in case you or maybe one of the other girls wants to get in touch with me."

She folded the paper, slipped it inside the cigarette pack's cellophane wrapper. Ten chances to one it'd be thrown away with the empty pack, but those odds were all I had. I'd take them.

On my way home, I called the number Serras had given me.

"Serras."

"LeGrande." I answered as an equal. "What's the current status on the Devine case?" Lesson I learned long ago—fake it and most people will follow your lead.

"We're about to crack it wide open, doll face."

Serras wasn't most people. He was police.

"You find any family?"

The pause told me Serras was deciding exactly where I fit in. Not easy to waylay a cop. They're paid to see right through you.

"How 'bout you?" He came back at me.

"What about me?"

"You got something for me? You learn anything at the Oyster you'd like to share?"

So they were cruising the Oyster. Good for them, although the manpower and case's stature wouldn't let it go on for more than a day or two.

"Yeah, I got a lecture on 'life is a bitch' from a chicken-legged number named Lucy."

He chuckled. "You're one up on us."

"Trying to make me feel better?"

"No."

I hadn't thought so. I debated telling him about the phone call Della had made. Only because he'd tucked Della in as if wishing her sweet dreams.

"I did learn one thing." Or maybe because I remembered his backside rumba and appreciated the effort. Still I was going to make him bite. A girl had to have standards.

Two seconds of silence passed until I heard "I'm here."

I'd take it. "Della was heard making plans to meet someone after work."

Another silence. "And?"

"That's it."

Serras wasn't the type to sigh. He was the type to swear. Professionalism prevented him from doing either. Maybe Billie was wrong. Maybe Serras had decided to play by the rules. Damn waste of man if that was the case.

"I appreciate the vital information, Ms. Le-Grande."

He had a right to sound sarcastic. The tip had lost something in the translation. Still it was something for an ex-stripper, dyslexic, college coed on her first murder case.

"What do you got for me?"

He chuckled. He was warming up.

"There was a brother—"

"I knew that by lunch." I took a turn at the sarcasm.

"Then you know he was recently killed."

"A train hit him."

"Investigation ruled it an accident."

"This one won't be so neat and tidy, though, will it, Detective?

"We're trying to locate the grandmother through Social Services. If the adoption was never formal, there'll be no formal record of it.

We did find the victim's birth record. No history found yet on the name listed under father."

"What about the mother?"

"Last-known address showed nothing. No other listing has come up yet. She might have remarried, moved away. We're still looking."

"So far, a dead end, then?"

He shouldn't have hesitated.

"C'mon, Serras, I gave you something." I said it as if I believed that would work.

"You gave me nothing, LeGrande."

"Okay, if I do find out something more, you get it first. Deal?"

"What exactly is your interest here?"

"Emergency contact."

I liked his laugh.

"All right. One of the neighbors saw a guy leaving the victim's apartment this morning. We ran the description of the man and the make of the car. We're talking to him now."

"Who is he?"

Serras didn't answer.

"I could know him. Might know something about him that you guys could use."

I was thinking up another lure to get Serras to give up the information when he said, "Name is Paul Chumsky."

It was my turn to pause.

"You know him?"

"Sort of."

Serras waited. I was becoming impressed by the man's patience.

"I was married to him."

Chapter Three

I figure everyone is entitled to one major mistake per lifetime. Mine was Paul Chumsky.

I got to the station and found Serras. He was looking as if he should have one of those warning stickers on him: Caution: Extremely Flammable Contents. May Spontaneously Ignite. Obviously Serras didn't like surprises.

"You were married to Paul Chumsky?"

"I kept my own name." Nobody queues up for strippers named Silver Chumsky. "You think Paul had something to do with Della's death?"

"We're asking him a few questions."

Della may have been on a downward spiral, and Paul could have been riding shotgun, but murder? It wasn't Paul's style. Too messy. The final residue of the matrimonial sacrament kicked in. "Paul's not a murderer."

A drunk, yes. An unfaithful husband, definitely.

"That's what he says. Says the victim and he had dinner at her place before her shift. She suggested he hang out. If it was a slow night, she'd get off early and they could get together back at the apartment. She'd give him a call from the club."

"You already knew she was planning on meeting someone after work?" So much for my hot tip.

"I figured you were trying to impress me."

"Would it be that easy?"

"No." Serras's glance told me I was getting under his skin. At this point, a win-win situation any way I looked at it.

"Said he waited at her apartment. Said he was pretty tired."

Interpretation: Paul's happy hour had started at noon instead of three. Youth, brashness and a slightly above-average talent had gotten my ex-husband to the semipro golf circuit, but he'd lacked the discipline and true genius to go further. When I met him, he'd had one mediocre season and knew it was his last. When I found myself pregnant, he proposed to me in what I always figured was one last desperate stab at immortality. He wasn't with me when I lost the baby, but when I told him, it was the first time I'd seen a man cry. We lasted two years. We weren't friends but we weren't enemies. We just weren't meant to be. Last I heard he was the resident pro over at the Meadows, a country club for Memphis moneybags. An ex-stripper with an ex-husband who's an ex-semipro. If life were a tic-tac-toe game, I'd have it made.

"Claims he must've fallen asleep because next thing he remembers is waking up on Ms. Devine's divan."

A cop who could be cute. Serras was getting under my skin.

"He doesn't remember anything else."

Since my husband's idea of sobriety is adding lime to his tequila shooters, for once he could be telling the truth. Blackouts can do that to you. I knew.

"He has a lawyer?" Ex or not, the man had rights—just not in my bed anymore.

"He hasn't been charged with anything yet."

Police lingo for "no evidence." "You've got nothing to hold him?"

"He's got no alibi."

"And no motive."

"He's nervous. He put in a call to Michael Kingsley's office. They sent an associate down to hold his hand."

I raised an eyebrow. Michael Kingsley was a high-priced mouthpiece to white-collar criminals. Not washed-up golf semipros.

"So, maybe Della's murder is more than an unfortunate incident?"

"Let's just say, your ex-husband has already phoned for a ride home."

"Can I see him?"

"Why?"

Cops. Always a question. "Catch up on old times."

Five foot eleven ex-strippers. Always an answer.

Serras cocked his head toward the benches in the hall on either side of the front desk. "You can wait, but he might be a while."

"Not if Michael Kingsley has his back and you guys have nothing on him but a sleepover."

Serras assessed me with a lean gaze and looking as good as an underwear ad. "What's your stake in this, LeGrande?"

I tried to decide if behind that hooded gaze I was a suspect. "You mean besides the fact my ex-husband was sleeping with a friend of mine who was murdered last night?"

He added another weapon. Silence.

Suddenly I felt truly tired. "Maybe it's just a small, small world after all, Serras."

A door opened. A group of men came into the hall. I saw Paul before he saw me. He was tan, fit, looking like a vote for the charmed life except for the puffiness around his eyes and a viciousness in his gaze that only a hangover and being held by the police could cause.

"Somebody else here to give you a ride, Chumsky." Serras said as the group approached.

"Popular fellow," one of the cops in the group remarked.

Paul turned, gave me the good smile that told me I'd already given him a ride. I didn't smile back. Being reminded what a chump I'd been makes me testy.

My ex-husband dismissed his hotshot lawyer and came toward me. He stood too close. The viciousness left his face. "Hey." His voice was low and for a moment, I forgave myself for falling in love with him once. I turned my head as he leaned toward me. His mouth fell onto my hair instead of my flesh with its still-intact nerve endings. I can be suckered by dogs, children and fools—but at least I know it.

"Good to see you still care, Silver," he murmured into my hair.

"Don't go getting all sloppy on me, Paul. What do you know about Della's death?" I whispered.

"Nothing."

I pulled away.

"Heard you got a new gig, Silver."

Yeah. Emergency contact. I glanced at Serras and the others watching us.

Paul turned to them. "Am I done here, gentlemen?"

"Make sure you stay where we can find you, Chumsky," a cop built like a side of beef said.

Paul raked his gaze over the cop, stopping at the skinny red scratches on his forearms. "She must have been a hellcat."

The cop took a step. Serras put a halting hand on the man's arm, across the scratches.

"Take your ex-husband home, LeGrande," Serras advised.

I pushed Paul toward the door. We reached the exit, stepped out into the moist heat.

"Still the charmer." I gave him that much.

"It's a gift."

"Pretty impressive legal counsel."

"Kingsley plays at the club. I cut ten strokes off his game. He's grateful." Paul smiled. If an actor, he would have been cast as a gigolo or a second-rate hood. "You look good, Silver."

"I didn't come here for compliments."

"Why did you come here?"

Good question.

"Feeling guilty?"

That's the problem with marriage. People get to know you.

"You're not responsible for Della's death, Silver."

"Then who is?"

"The police are trying to find out."

"Della was a stripper who snorted in her off hours. The only family that has come up was run over by a train several months ago. They won't even have her buried before the case comes off the role call, and you know it."

"Listen, all I can tell you is Della and I used to get together, have a few laughs. Yesterday afternoon, we'd gotten together. She said she was going to try and get off early at the club. Why not stick around? I waited. When she didn't call, I fell asleep."

I stopped short. "Della didn't call you?"

Paul gave me the same patient look he'd given me the first time I'd told him I wanted a divorce.

"It's been a long day, Silver. C'mon, we'll pick up my car, and I'll buy you some dinner."

"One of the girls that worked at the Oyster overheard Della make a phone call last night from the club to meet someone after work."

"She probably did call me. I fell asleep and didn't hear the phone."

"Was there a message on her answering machine this morning?"

"Now that you mention it, it was beeping."

He was lying. That marriage-getting-to-know-someone deal is a two-way street.

"C'mon." He smiled. "You can interrogate me over Italian."

Translation: pasta for me, a bottle of burgundy for Paul. But he was hiding something and I wanted to know what. I stretched out my rubber band to the point of breaking, let it go.

"Dino's is still good," I suggested.

"Fine," Paul agreed. Food wasn't his primary concern anyway.

We headed to my car. Paul folded himself into the compact. "How's Aunt Peggilee?" He put on the country club charm.

"She's at Margarita Mania at the Elks."

Paul went all teeth. "She's a live one, your aunt Peggilee."

I had to agree.

"I thought Della was yanking my chain when she told me you left Billie's for higher education."

His sidelong gaze told me he was picturing me in a short plaid pleated skirt and loafers with ankle socks. Paul liked fantasy in and out of the bedroom.

"She might have been yanking some things of yours, but that was the truth. When you'd two get together anyway?"

"Met up with her one night at Silky's downtown about six months ago. She was finishing her night. I was just starting mine." He looked out over the dash. "Two old friends, that's all. She'd call me every now and then. If I was free, we'd get together, have a few drinks, a few laughs." He looked at me. "When's the last you'd seen her?"

I steered into a one-way street. "A while."

"She'd mention you now and then. She was all gung-ho on getting out herself."

"Leaving Billie's to go to the Oyster wasn't exactly the direct route."

We picked up his car. I insisted on separate cars. He followed me to the restaurant. Inside, the dim lights and the candles flicking in Chianti bottles made all the waiters look soulful. We were ushered to a round table for two. I ordered eggplant; Paul ordered a bottle of burgundy. I began another bruise on my wrist.

"After her brother's death…" Paul shook his head. "Della wasn't having an easy time with it."

"Billie told me about it. Said police ruled it an accident."

Paul said nothing, watched for the wine.

"Auntie says there is no such thing as an accident."

The wine came with the bread.

"Is that what you think?" Paul tasted the wine. Satisfaction smoothed out his face.

I shrugged. "All I know is Della's dead, and a few months earlier her brother dies also."

Paul took another large swallow. "Coincidence."

"Auntie doesn't believe in coincidence, either."

Paul smiled closemouthed, raised his glass. "To Auntie."

"How was Della really, Paul?"

"You know Della. She always liked a good time, but when I caught up with her, after her brother's death…" he stopped, drank. "Sometimes it stops being fun."

Been there. Paul had never left. Della had. The hard way.

"Did she talk about it? Her brother's death?"

"No." He poured another glass of wine, drank half of it. I pushed the basket of bread toward him. He ignored it.

"She never said anything about it?"

I met his gaze hard. His pupils dilated. Could be the booze. Or he could be lying. Both, I decided.

"Maybe, once in awhile. After a night of it, when the speed was wearing off but the shakes hadn't set in yet. Problem with junkies. If they don't cut it with booze, they get high-strung."

My ex-husband, lifestyle coach.

"What'd she say?"

He waved his glass. "The usual."

"What would that be?"

"How unfair it was, what a good kid he was, how it should have been her," Paul singsonged.

Last night it was, I thought. The waiter set my antipasto before me. I popped a cherry tomato, chewed a hot pepper until tears blurred my gaze. My ex-husband drank. Things were beginning to blur for him, too.

"Why do you think she wanted to see you last night?"

I received the choice smile that put him in the good graces of the country club's male members and in the firm beds of their wives. "The usual."

This time I didn't have to ask him for a definition. Our meals came. Paul ordered another bottle of wine, pushed the pasta around his plate. I hadn't eaten all day. I finished my salad, entree and several more breadsticks, heartened by the return of my normal, lusty appetite. Obsessions seem to revolve around three main categories—drugs, sex or food—and presently the last one was the safest for me. Fortunately, at thirty-one, my five-foot-eleven frame with one-eighty curves could handle it for now although I knew it was only a matter of time before things would spread and soften and I'd be left with cats and cross-stitch and the weekly tabloids for relief.

I ordered espresso, Paul a double brandy. Paul was a drunk but he wasn't a sloppy drunk. I'd never seen him get abusive or belligerent. He just sat up straighter, and I could tell by that gleam in his eyes he believed himself somebody significant. Paul couldn't have murdered Della Devine.

I finished my espresso, caught the waiter's eye.

"Another, ma'am?"

"You can bring the check."

"No rush." My ex-husband handed his glass to the waiter.

"Another double, sir?"

Paul nodded. "Have another espresso, Silver. It's not often we get together."

"That would be because we're divorced." I shook my head at the waiter. He left to get Paul's drink.

"Not by my choice."

I pushed my chair from the table. "I've got an early class tomorrow."

"And I've got an early tee time. One more drink and then we'll go."

It was an old refrain, one I'd sung often before, too. Still Della was dead, my ex-husband was a drunk and my dreams were as tenuous as the rubber band on my wrist.

The waiter returned. "Give me another espresso," I ordered. "Make it a double," I decided, sounding cavalier, feeling crazed.

Paul's smile said, "That's my girl."

Old husbands like old habits are hard to break.

An hour and a half later, careening on caffeine and Paul unsteady when he stood, we walked to our cars. He'd set his keys on the table when he'd taken out his wallet to pay the bill. I'd lifted them when he'd gone to the men's room. He was patting his pockets now.

"C'mon, Paul, I'll give you a ride home. You can pick up your car in the morning."

He opened his mouth to protest.

"I'll swing by before class, give you a ride."

"No need. Just sleep over."

A drunk is bad enough. A leering drunk was pure sorrow. I might never need another rubber band again. "Let's get you home."

"The night's young, Silver."

He was right. Eleven forty-five was when the fun began in the clubs. I continued to my car. I looked back. Paul wasn't following me.

He shrugged, gave me a thin smile. "An empty house. An empty bed."

An empty bottle, I thought.

"I'm going to hang out a little longer. Give me my keys."

"You're in no shape to drive."

"Sweet that you care, honey, but you aren't responsible for me any longer."

"That doesn't mean I won't feel guilty if something happens to you." I unlocked my car and got in. I rolled down the window.

"Admit it. You still care, Sterling." He used my favorite nickname.

"One funeral per week is my limit." I started the car. "Last chance."

He came toward the car, although I knew he wasn't coming with me. He was beyond persuasion. He leaned down. "Give me a kiss good-bye."

I took it on the mouth this time. I felt he deserved that much. I watched him walk away, the man I'd once legally vowed to love. He headed toward a neon martini glass with a winking olive.

I WOKE WITH a caffeine headache. Auntie was sitting at the kitchen table with her soy milk and muttering to herself over the day's stock market report. I poured a cup of black coffee. In for a penny, in for a pound. She let me take a sip before she asked with a skinny gaze, "Where were you last night?"

"Not shimmying to salsa." Caffeine headache or not, I was mean in the morning. I sat down, instantly contrite. "Sorry."

"Honey, you think I pay any mind to you in the morning? I know you're ornerier than a gut-shot she-boar. It don't faze me none, because you get it from me. Carl burped at the breakfast table one morning over fried eggs, and I stuck my fork in his arm. It stood right up on its own. Had to change his Sunday shirt and we were late for ten-o'clock service. Had to tiptoe and squeeze in next to Loretta Knolls with her big behind and her husband who smelled of pork fat. Carl didn't burp at the breakfast table ever again."

Carl was Aunt Peggilee's third husband. Matrimonial mistakes are another thing I inherited from the LeGrande women. Except Momma, who said she loved men too much to marry one. As I get older, Momma gets wiser to me.

"You'll mellow with the years, Silver."

I rubbed my forehead.

"Rough night?" Aunt Peggilee's gaze was on my black-and-blue wrist.

"Paul was seen leaving Della's apartment yesterday morning. The police picked him up for questioning. I went down to the precinct. We had dinner."

Aunt Peggilee shook her head, her beehive wobbling and threatening to give way. "Silver, Silver," was all she said, but she looked at me like I was a calf being led to slaughter.

I took a swallow of coffee. "He drank to you."

"The man would toast Beelzebub himself if it meant a good gulp."

Must have been the fact I'd been foolish enough to marry him that made me feel compelled to defend him. "A lot of gals have done a lot worse." It was a weak argument, but it was all I had.

"Silver, don't get me wrong. I don't mind the man myself. I just mind him with you."

"He's not *with* me. We had pasta together."

Auntie raised an eyebrow.

"Okay, I had pasta. He had several bottles of red. He and Della had been running into each other—"

"Like Mack trucks, I imagine." Auntie took a delicate sip of soy milk.

"And I wanted to talk to him about her."

Auntie eyed me over her glass. "Did you learn anything?"

I shrugged. "Pretty much what I expected. She was really shook up by her brother's death and in a bad way."

Aunt Peggilee studied me. "It's not your fault, Silver."

"I know. I just don't know why…" I shook my head, too much caffeine and too little sleep making me sappy. "I wish I'd called her. Or she'd gotten in touch with me."

Auntie Peggilee put her hand on mine, squeezed. "She did, honey."

I DRANK ANOTHER CUP of coffee while I dressed. I went to my underwear drawer, opened a small box next to a dried-out honeysuckle sachet and took out an elastic. A new day, a new rubber band. I closed the drawer, picked up Paul's keys from my dresser top. I jangled them. Besides his car keys, there were others, house keys, office keys, a smaller one that probably opened a locker. I dropped the keys into my purse on the kitchen counter and grabbed two Tootsie Pops out of the cupboard. I locked up, Auntie having left for breakfast bingo and Adrienne knocking off a despised but required phys ed credit with an early-morning fencing class. I started the car, got the air conditioner blasting. I unwrapped one pop, stuck it in my mouth and headed out.

By the time I'd gotten to my second candy-coated chewy center, I'd called Paul on my cell phone twice to tell him I was on my way but there was no answer. If I couldn't rouse him before Macro, I'd leave the keys, and he could call a cab.

Paul lived in a small but well-designed modern home on the edge of one of the tony neighborhoods. Tips on the greens had gotten good.

I went to the back door, didn't even bother to knock, twisted the doorknob before pawing through my purse for the keys. The door clicked open. The house had a security system, but the alarm hadn't been activated. Liquor might make the old pathetic but it gave the young a sense of invincibility. Paul, at thirty-five, was on the cusp.

I called out hello, not expecting an answer. "Paul?"

The back door opened into a kitchen with stainless steel appliances whose constant reflection would make a woman past forty take a sharp object to their surface, but was a perfect panorama for a premiddle-age country-club pro. The room was arranged for a *House Beautiful* spread, the uneven trio of chairs around the table instead of the expected four the only touch of whimsy. Paul was a fastidious housekeeper. I'd watched him cotton swab a heating grate once for twenty minutes and still didn't understand. Funny the things that endear a person to you.

As I walked into a spacious, open living room with a vaulted ceiling, I saw the bleached white briefs first. Directly eye level, Fruit of the Loom, waist size thirty-two. Paul always wore Fruit of the Loom, waist size thirty-two. Mundane details such as these allowed me to step toward the body in the white briefs hanging from the ceiling rafters.

"Damn." I fumbled for my phone in my purse as I ran into the kitchen. I grabbed a knife from the end of the built-in butcher-block cutting board, found my phone as I ran back into the living room, dialed 911. "Damn," I told the woman's voice as I righted the missing kitchen chair under Paul's dangling body in the spotless white underwear. I climbed onto the chair.

"Ma'am, do you need…"

As I reached high for the rope, I saw the red

garter necktie with the gold double *D* around Paul's throat. I sawed at the rope with the knife.

"Ma'am..."

The body spun full circle. I looked down from the rope, directly into Paul's dead eyes, sputtered the only other recent savior I'd met. "Serras."

I sawed harder, my weight pushing against the body. The body swung back. I lost my balance. The chair tipped. The phone dropped from the tuck in my shoulder. I clutched Paul's red-gartered neck with the gold double *D* charm, wrapping my legs around his hips in a position that we'd actually both been quite fond of in our past. We twirled Cirque du Soleil for several seconds, then our weight ripped us loose. We went down, me clinging to my dead ex-husband as if climaxing. My head struck something hard, sharp. *Until death do us part.* Hell, like I'd ever meant that literally. Down I went into darkness.

Chapter Four

I woke to a civil servant with a gun and Apollo ancestry hovering over me. I hadn't gone to heaven yet. But it wasn't quite hell, either.

Serras looked down at me. "Silver LeGrande. Everybody's favorite emergency contact."

I mustered a grimace as I attempted to gain a vantage point by rising. The marching band in my head made the worst morning-after I'd ever experienced seem like a Sunday in the park. Cymbals clashed along my frontal lobe, laid me low again. Serras's eyes narrowed as if he'd heard them, too.

"Easy," he said. One of the ambulance attendants flashed him a dirty glance, no one certain who Serras spoke to. I liked to think all of us. I looked past him. The area around the scene was being secured. A cop was sketching the room. Another was photographing the corpse from different angles. I winced as the Polaroid flashed.

The attendants' hands were gentle as they rolled me onto a stretcher. Yet my body stiffened. They strapped me in. My eyes met Serras's as I was lifted.

Easy.

With the hope of intravenous pain killer and the gaze of my newfound Greek-god-guru, I let myself be carried away. The stretcher began to roll. Serras began to walk. He was carrying my purse.

"You assigned to hold my hand?" I like to play it tough when I'm feeling tender.

"You called me, remember?"

"I'm getting the idea you're not going to let me forget."

Past Serras, a cop knelt down to examine the marks on my dead ex-husband's neck. Paul's handsome face was discolored, distorted. His eyes were frozen as if still seeing his killer.

"You going to find out who did this to him?"

Serras baited me with one arched brow. Behind the skepticism, the gears were shifting. A dead junkie stripper. Maybe it had been an accident in the carnival of carnal excess, maybe it had been deliberate, a game of rough-and-tumble gone too far. Didn't much matter because obviously the guilty party had gone straight for atonement by leaping off his dinette chair. Murder-suicide. Wrap a red bow around it, and another day of detective work well done.

"Sometimes a cigar is more than a cigar, Serras." Even Monica Lewinsky had her moments. So did I as I got a grin from Serras. The attendants slid me into the back of the ambulance. The door slammed on Serras. The attendants were fussing, checking pulse, heartbeat, breath. I closed my eyes. Della and Paul stared back at me. Blank, vacant gazes.

"Hey." I opened my eyes to the attendant leaning over me. "Someone murders someone but wants to make it look like suicide. How could they slip up?"

The attendant got a gleam in his eye as if about to administer pure oxygen.

"Say we're talking about what happened back there. Say the victim was strangled first, then hung. How would you know?"

The attendant's expression turned matter-of-fact. "There would be two sets of marks. If the victim was strangled with a rope or cord—"

"Garter belt," I interrupted, remembering the red satin strip around Paul's neck, the double *D* gold charm swaying delicately along his Adam's apple."

"Sure, anything like that. There would be a bruise in a straight line circling the neck." The attendant drew a slash along his own throat. "Probably also a big bruise at the back of the neck where usually the most pressure is exerted. Now, if the victim was strangled with bare hands, usually you see signs of struggle, internal and external damage to the neck. Many times too much force is used. The contusions, abrasions are more severe."

Silver thought of Della. The line around her neck had been straight, tidy.

"But the marks on the neck from a hanging are different. The rope causes an inverted vee on the neck." The attendant drew the shape in the air as if conducting a symphony.

I tried to concentrate past the cacophony in my brain. The red garter, the red pinpoints of blood vessels, Paul's eyes bulging as if he'd walked into a surprise party. Which he obviously had. Surprise of his life.

My head throbbed.

At the emergency room, I was poked and prodded, stitched up, told to take over-the-counter ibuprofen for any discomfort and thrown back into the melee of society without sympathy. Waiting to catch me was Serras, leaning against a wall, arms crossed, wearing an expression the English comp T.A. would phrase "sardonic."

I moved in to a dangerous foot away from being in his face. "Got the killer yet?"

"Which one?" He didn't smile.

"The one who seems fond of strangling my friends."

His eyebrow arched. Sardonic to the soul.

"That's your theory? Your ex-husband was strangled by someone and strung up to make it look like suicide? His tone didn't say whether he was buying it or not.

"Were the bruises on his neck in an upside-down *V*?" I imitated the ambulance attendant's maestro move.

Serras's expression didn't change. *Not easily impressed,* I was reminded.

"Or was there a bruise in a straight line beneath the garter belt, circling the neck?" Christ, my voice actually sounded hopeful.

"C'mon." Serras put his hand on the small of my back in another of those unexpected gestures that could mess a gal up royally. I stepped away from his touch.

"I'll drive you over to pick up your car."

"What's the official word, Serras? Paul murdered Della, then took his own life?"

Serras's dark eyes were on me, taking me in

beneath twin sharp brows. I suspected his lips' clean line of contempt was natural rather than mastered like most cops. He didn't even have to open them. I knew. He wasn't going to tell me a damn thing.

"That's one theory." He stopped at a standard-issue squad sedan.

"What's yours?" I ignored the door he'd pulled open. I'd learned long ago height had its advantages.

His gaze would have given another whiplash. I was glad I'd planted my feet. "Get in, LeGrande."

I didn't move. Neither did he. Yet he seemed to loom larger. Neat optical illusion. "You've got to give me something, Serras."

His mouth jerked up at the corners. If nothing else, his amusement was worth the effort…and enough to give me encouragement.

"Why?"

I used a shoulder roll I'd often employed on stage. "Tit for tat." If his gaze so much as flickered in the direction of my notable bosom, it was all over between us.

His gaze stayed its intimidating course. My illusions remained intact, a rare claim for someone of my age and colorful background. I grew grateful. Maybe Serras was one of the good guys after all.

"I did have dinner with Paul last night. Was probably one of the last people to see him alive," I reminded, my voice going to a soft lull of insinuation.

Serras gave me the flat look that was probably a course itself at the academy. Nothing in his face flinched. Give this guy a table in Vegas and he'd clean up. I waited for the obstruction-of-justice spiel.

"You like to play with big boys, LeGrande?" In the scheme of things, he had the power. We both knew it. Yet so far, he hadn't pulled any trump cards. My estimation of him went a little higher. Also made me worry what he was saving them for.

"Two people I know dead in two days, Serras. Doesn't exactly put me in the mood for pinochle."

His lips twisted into a smirk, confirming I sounded like the bad-B-movie imitation I'd imagined. "I can either give you a ride or call someone to pick you up." If the man was hungry for what I might know, he wasn't showing it.

"When did I become your responsibility, Serras?"

"Civic duty. Comes with the cool car." The smirk was faint but there. I didn't make a move. The smirk widened into a smile as if he appreciated a good standoff.

"C'mon, I'll buy you a cup of coffee, LeGrande, and you can spill your guts."

"You think that's all it takes?"

"You found your ex-husband strung up like a piñata and got a nice headache yourself in the process." He reached over and brushed the strands of hair away from the four stitches above my temple. "I'd say it's the best offer you've had today."

I slid into the car. Best offer I'd had in years, but Serras would have to stick around a little longer than a double latte to find that out.

He pulled into a diner not far from the hospital. We settled across from each other in a high-backed booth. The waitress slapped two menus on the laminated table.

"Coffee?" She asked automatically.

We nodded. She turned over the thick white ceramic cups on the table and filled them with the pot she had brought with her. "I'll be back in a moment to get your orders." She moved on to another table.

I added several sugars and creams to my coffee. Without adding anything, Serras raised his cup to his lips.

"I bet you used to smoke, too." I swirled cream into my cup.

He smiled above the rising steam. "Pack and a half a day."

"What made you quit?" I tested my coffee, reached for another packet of sugar.

"I decided there were better ways to kill myself." He heard his words. "Sorry."

"I'm an ex-stripper, Serras. I'm not exactly renowned for my refined sensibilities."

The waitress returned, pen poised above her pad. "What'll you have?"

"Hungry?" Serras's expression revealed nothing, but I decided I was making progress getting past his professionally honed defenses.

I shook my head. He ordered the number three special with an extra side of ham.

"Paul didn't kill himself," I said as soon as the waitress was out of earshot.

He sipped his coffee. "Then someone sure went to a lot of trouble to make it look that way." He eased back against the bench seat. "Okay, what's your take?" He said as if doing me the favor.

I propped my elbows on the table and leaned in. "I'm not a morning person to begin with, Serras. Imagine the funk I'm in today. Don't patronize me."

"I didn't bring you here because of your bubbly personality, LeGrande."

I came in closer. "You think Paul was murdered, too?"

The arrival of the number three special with a side of ham interrupted the conversation. The waitress aimed a teeth-baring smile at Serras. "What else can I do for you?"

"This is fine for the moment, thank you." Serras picked up a knife and fork, paused to look at me before digging into order number three. "No signs of struggle. Nothing was taken. No evidence anyone else was there, let alone broke in. The crime scene will do a full report, but the preliminary findings all say it was suicide. What makes you so sure your ex-husband didn't kill himself?"

I relaxed back, adopting an easiness I was far from feeling. "Not his style. Paul preferred to do it slow, leisurely. One drink at a time."

Serras stabbed his egg with a toast triangle. He sopped up the yolk with the bread. He ate with obvious pleasure. The man had a lusty appetite. I sensed it extended to other areas besides eating.

He gave me the ol' one-brow lift. Its angle said, That's it? *Not easily impressed*, I remembered.

The waitress returned with the coffeepot. I let her fill my cup, added sugars and cream, stirred nonchalantly before I raised my eyes to his.

"What happened after you and your ex-husband left the station last night?"

I steadied my gaze on him. "C'mon, give it up. You don't think it was suicide, either, do you?"

"Let's see what the M.E. finds out. In the meantime, why don't you tell me what happened last night?"

"If you guys had had surveillance on him, we wouldn't be having this conversation," I challenged.

He speared a sausage link, popped it whole into his mouth and chewed while contemplating me. Finally he swallowed and said, "How do you know we didn't? Maybe I'm just making sure we didn't miss something." He stabbed another sausage. "Maybe I just didn't feel like eating breakfast alone."

"My great-aunt once stuck a fork in her husband's arm because he burped at the breakfast table." I moved in and in a cut-the-crap tone, warned, "Like I said, Serras, LeGrande women aren't morning people."

He smiled. Mr. Sardonic. "You're trying to

tell me your mood was better last night when you left with your ex-husband?"

I eyed the silverware he'd slid out of my reach. "We picked up Paul's car, went to Dino's off of Jackson. Separate cars. I ate, Paul drank. I took his keys, offered to drive him home. He wasn't ready to call it a night."

"You didn't give him back his keys?"

"No. I'd already seen enough death for one day, thank you. Gave him one last chance, he refused. I told him I'd stop by in the morning, pick him up and give him a ride to his car." I reached for my coffee cup. "You know the rest." The memory of the morning after fell on me as if to flatten me. My hands threatened to shake. I put down the coffee cup and was thoroughly disgusted with myself.

"Did your ex-husband talk about his relationship with Ms. Devine?"

Again Serras's formal use of Della's stage name was not lost on me. If he was trying to get into my good graces, it was working.

"Sure, he said he ran into her one night at a place downtown about six months ago. Della and I were pretty close at one time. For some of that time I was married to Paul."

Serras cleaned the last of the egg yolk from the plate, pushed the plate away from him and signaled the waitress for coffee. "What happened?"

"I stopped drinking. He didn't. We got divorced."

Serras smiled thinly. "I meant between you and Ms. Devine?"

"Nothing happened. I left the club. She didn't. We didn't see each other every day any longer. She wasn't tough, Della. They probably ate her up alive at the Oyster." I sat on my hands as they began to shake. I glanced at the wall clock as if I had someplace to be.

"You looked out for her."

"Most knew not to mess with Billie's girls but on occasion…" I took a long breath. "She could act the act, but she was a kid. A screwed-up kid who didn't stand a chance." I slid my hands free from beneath my backside. Under the table I gave the elastic a good snap. *Straighten up.*

"Who looked out for you?"

The guy threw a good curve. I flattened my hands on the tabletop as if about to lay out my terms. "I did."

He tapped my wrist. "What's this?"

"A rubber band."

"Yesterday's was blue. Today's is red."

Detectives and details. Like peanut butter and jelly. "Depends on my mood."

"Why do you wear one on your wrist all the time?"

"Secret weapon."

"Against what?" His eyes held mine.

"Against losing control."

"You don't like losing control, LeGrande?"

"I like to say when and where."

He leaned back, smiled as if he liked me. "Was your ex-husband depressed?"

It took me a minute to catch up. I suspected the sudden shift in conversation was deliberate on Serras's part. I sharpened my gaze. "Paul? He was the life of every party."

"Was that what last night was? A party?"

"Paul preferred a light touch to life. Depression was too strenuous."

We both shook our heads as the waitress approached with the coffeepot. She set down the pot, ripped off the check from a pad in her pocket, slapped it facedown on the table and gave Serras another grand grin before moving on.

"Did you and your ex-husband argue?"

"Last night?" He'd caught me off guard again.

"Any night."

I gave him a cool shrug. "What married couple doesn't?"

"Besides his drinking, did your husband have any other bad habits?"

"You mean other women?"

Serras waited. I leaned in low. "Don't you think if I was going to murder Paul, I would have done it when we were married and he was sleeping with the upper east side of Memphis."

"Your ex-husband slept with female members of the country club?"

"My ex-husband believed in customer service." I relaxed back. "But if you and your pals are worth a fraction of the taxpayers' money, you already knew that before my anesthesia wore off."

Serras neither confirmed nor denied. He was playing it close to the chest.

"You're wasting your time here, Detective. We weren't exactly Ozzie and Harriet, but no matter what Paul did during the course of our ill-fated marriage, I'd never wish him dead."

Serras threw some bills on the table. I slid out of the booth.

"So what exactly was your ex-husband's relationship with Ms. Devine?"

"He said they'd get together now and then. Have a party."

"Private parties?"

"I'm sure they did it at least once or twice in

the coat checkroom at a club downtown just for kicks."

Serras gave a low chuckle. "That's good, Le-Grande, but c'mon, that's all you got for me?"

"For now," I alluded.

He leveled a look my way. "You wouldn't be thinking of going into my line of work, now would you?"

"I'm an ex-stripper, Serras. I've already had my share of glamour professions."

DELLA'S BODY was released Tuesday. The funeral was on Thursday. I failed my macro exam on Wednesday.

Thursday morning I slipped on a black sheath that did double duty as my dinner date dress. Dinner dates, funerals. Sometimes there was only a thin line.

My fingers shook as I tried to clasp the gold cross around my throat. I muttered a curse, slammed the necklace on the bureau. I held my hands out in front of me. They trembled like a virgin's thighs. I opened the top dresser drawer, stretched two elastics onto my wrist. Definitely a double-rubber-band day.

It was a thin group at church. If Della had had any surviving family, they hadn't been found. Billic was footing the bill and sat ringside, her face shiny, dark and solemn. I recognized many of my ex-co-workers, but a lot of the faces were unfamiliar. Some were probably from the Oyster. Others I had the suspicion were employees Billie had persuaded with a strong arm to show at the service even if they hadn't known Della. Billie believed in a packed house. She had done her best, but there were still too many empty seats.

Serras came in, turned out in a gray pinstripe. He sat down beside me without invitation, scanned the crowd before giving me a nod. He unbuttoned his suit jacket. I saw a flash of the standard-issue Glock before he shifted. I slid over in the pew to make more room for him and banged into Auntie who was giving Serras her serious roving eye. I was glad to see him. His presence meant the department was taking Della's death seriously.

Serras nodded at Auntie. She leaned over me, the scent of Aquanet Extra Hold strong.

"Did you know the deceased?" Auntie whispered.

"No," Serras answered. "Did you?"

"No." Auntie leaned back. "So, that's the dick?" she whispered to me out of the side of her mouth. Auntie was a fan of Raymond Chandler.

"That's the dick," I answered.

Serras continued to survey the room. I followed his lead. Faces looked wan and puffy in the morning light. Tears were few. It took a lot to make a stripper cry in public. The service was brief and impersonal, the sunlight deepening the stained-glass windows offering little comfort. There would be no graveside service. The attendees filed out, slipping on sunglasses against the perverse sunshine, concealing their blank expressions. They stood in small groups, not knowing whether to leave or stay. They smoked with shallow, nervous drags on slim cigarettes, speaking in undertones with abrupt flutters of their hands. I hugged several of the girls I'd worked with at Billie's. Some went stiff in my arms. I'd seen their glances inside, the rolling eyes of some of the resentful who wondered what right I had to be there. Several looked thinner than I remembered. Some looked older. We'd been a boisterous group at Billie's. Today we talked in murmurs like the incessant sounds of small rodents running through walls, a paltry expression of "I exist, I exist."

Billie paused on the church's top step to survey the group. Her gaze settled on Serras, who'd already pulled loose his tie and unbuttoned his shirt collar. They nodded to each other as if partners. She glanced at her diamond watch cutting into her dimpled wrists. Beneath her we all had a hungry look. "The club will not be open for business today," she announced in her low contralto. "Come. Join me there to remember our colleague and friend." She added a gracious flourish of her small, plump hand so the invite seemed less like an order.

The groups split into smaller parts, moving toward cars. Billie came down the stairs with a feline grace and dark half-moons under her eyes. She moved to Serras, took his hand, whispered something to him as he leaned forward to kiss her offered cheek. He was smiling as he straightened. Fifty-five and easily 225 pounds naked, but she still had it. She knew it and so did we.

"Now you give me something to smile about, Lexi." Billie leaned her head to the side, her gaze thinning. "Who did this to my girl?"

"She wasn't your girl when she died, Billie."

"Who's girl was she then, my handsome friend?" Billie's soft lilt lingered in the silence.

"You keep a tight bead on the circuit. You know more about what goes on in any club within a fifty-mile radius than some of the owners do, darlin'."

Billie released a light breath, let her shoulders drop dramatically. "As you pointed out, *chère,* Della had left me. What you know I know."

"You said `your girl' had to be let go because of her untidy habits."

Billie gave Serras a shrewd look.

"M.E.'s report showed no traces of illegal substances. Della Devine was clean when she died."

Billie clicked her tongue against the roof of her mouth. "Normally that would be good news, *chère.*"

"Della had cleaned up her act?" I asked, a new sadness seeping into my rubbery bones.

"The toxicology reports showed no traces of drugs in her system."

"But even Paul had said Della was having a hard time between the drugs and the drinking."

Aunt Peggilee patted my arm. "Paul wasn't exactly a model of credibility, dear."

"He had no reason to lie." I looked at Serras. "Or murder Della and then take his own life."

The trio looked at me but withheld any pity. I wasn't certain why I was defending my cheating, alcoholic now-dead ex-husband. Maybe because I had once loved him. And he had loved me. Even if it'd gone sour, loving someone and being loved isn't something you turn your back on lightly.

Aunt Peggilee gave her gaze to Serras. "I don't suppose my niece's ex-husband's toxicology screens were clean."

"The report's not back yet."

"So she dried out, kicked it for a few days. Good for her," Billie said. "Shame this had to happen when she was on her way back up."

"But if Della's habit was as heavy as everyone claims, traces of the drug would have stayed in her system for over a month." I'd read the pamphlets. "If she was clean that long, it seems she was the only one who noticed it. What about the autopsy?"

"There was no autopsy." Serras offered no apology.

"What do you mean?" I straightened, ready to choose my weapons.

Billie laid a restraining hand on my forearm, her mandarin nails exerting pressure. She had known me a long time. "Come. They are waiting for us at the club. I need an absinthe. I suspect you do, too, my handsome friend," she spoke to Serras. "We will have a drink, and you will explain why Royce sent you only to appease me."

Chapter Five

Outside the Southern sun had shown no mercy, but inside Billie's it was cool and dim, the velvet drapes the purple of royalty drawn against the outside. The front door was locked. A handwritten sign that said Closed Today Due to Death in the Family had been propped in a window.

Billie had stayed true to her original inspiration for the club and decorated it in the rich colors of the Mardi Gras. Necklaces of metallic glass beads were strung across valances, weaved around candles, draped along gilt frames. The dominant deep purple was broken by green and gold, all reflecting on the warm tones of cherry wood. Black and white tiles contrasted like ermine collars and cuffs on sovereign robes.

We settled at the round table with the full view of the club that was always reserved for Billie. Billie placed a sugar cube on a slotted spoon held over a small glass of green liquid.

She drizzled ice water over the spoon, dissolving the sugar and turning the liquid milky. She smiled as she slid the drink to Auntie. She prepared her own. Serras opted for bourbon neat. I had chicory coffee with scalded milk.

Billie stood, raised her glass. At the tables and along the bar, all followed suit.

"To Della."

"To Della," echoed others.

Billie sat, took a deep sip, set down her glass and gazed at Serras.

"Royce didn't send me," he said.

Billie swirled the liquid in her glass. "Yet here you are. You are on the clock?"

"I'll fill out a call sheet."

"Memphis Homicide has decided Della's death was a crime of passion?"

"No official statement has been filed."

Billie gestured with her glass. I burned my tongue on the coffee. "No autopsy, no sanctioned department presence at the funeral. An official statement is not necessary."

"The investigation is ongoing."

Billie cupped the side of Serras's face. "Now you try to appease me, *chère*. Is it that bad?"

"A woman is strangled. A man who has admitted to being her sometimes lover is seen leaving her apartment. Twenty-four hours later he's found strung up beneath his skylight, an apparent suicide."

Billie tipped her glass, watching the liquid shift. "Again, here you are, *chère*." A smile curled her crimson lips. "Is it a slow day in Memphis?"

He sipped his drink. "I've never known one."

Billie's smile widened. She raised her glass, clinked it against his. "Thank you for coming, my handsome friend. It will not be forgotten." She rose. "Excuse me a moment. I must see about the food, my other guests." She glided away, stopped and leaned over the long bar to speak to the bartender. She pointed a long fingernail their way. The bartender nodded and began preparing another round of drinks for their table. Auntie stood also.

"Excuse me, children. I'll be right back." She headed in the direction of the rest rooms. Her eyes had been bright but her step was steady.

I found Serras's gaze on me. "So that's it?" I asked him. "A murder-suicide?"

"You tell me."

"I think the police are trying to pin this on Paul," I told him.

Serras sipped his drink, stayed silent.

"I think you think so, too.

His smile was slow. "You can read my mind now, LeGrande?"

"Honey." I gave him a pitying look as I patted his arm. "Big, silent lugs like you are my specialty."

He caught my hand, pulling me slightly toward him, leaned in, his voice low. "Tell me what I'm thinking now, LeGrande."

His grasp was firm but not painful, the kind of touch that made me want to hold on. I drew a breath, moved in even closer, felt his heat.

"You're thinking you had it all figured out. A gold shield, twenty years and then it's off to someplace far from the city streets where the only animals are the kind that scamper up your front porch steps for the bits of stale bread you left there for them. But along comes a couple of strippers, one dead, one alive, and you can feel it in your heart, Serras. All hell's about to break loose."

I disentangled my hand, leaned back. His half-lidded gaze gave me nothing. "It's why you slipped a Windsor knot around your neck this morning and came here. Just like me, you can smell it."

He eased back in the chair. "Smell what, LeGrande?"

"Something rotten."

He picked up his glass but didn't drink. "Did you know your ex-husband made you sole heir and executor of his will?"

He had hit me with the flat bottom of a frying pan. Worse, the bastard knew it. "Impressive, Detective." I picked up my coffee cup and saluted him, trying for my own version of cool and collected. "You've been dying to spring that on me all morning, yet here you sat, cool as a catfish in Cold Hollow Creek. Waiting...waiting..." I played with the words and played with Serras. "For the perfect moment. And you got it, didn't you."

"Control." He reached out, pulled back the blue rubber band on my wrist. "Nothing wrong with losing it as long as you can say when and where, right?" He released the elastic gently, slowly, no snap against my skin.

"Paul had a will?"

"We found it in a file box in his closet."

"Not very original."

Serras shrugged. "In matters such as this, common sense tends to supersede creativity."

I digested this pearl. I shook my head slowly from side to side. "You didn't know Paul."

The look Serras shot me asked if I had, either. With the doubt and questions reeling within my caffeine-rich brain, I had to give him that one.

"Practical matters, in fact, the whole reality shtick was not Paul's forte." I'd get an A in Freshman English yet.

"Maybe he'd decided to turn over a new leaf."

"Like Della?"

Serras eased back in his chair with all the time in the world. *You tell me,* his rock-your-socks mug said.

I considered the idea. Nah. "It was probably another token of gratitude from Kingsley. Lord, take ten strokes off a man's par and he becomes your love slave. And us strippers think *we* have a gig."

Serras released his smile as slowly as the rubber band. "His lawyer this time wasn't a glamour boy like Kingsley. Johnny Flint. Runs a one-man operation over Debrese's Specialty Meats on the south side. Specializes in ambulance chasing but the will is legit. Your ex-husband had it drawn up a few months ago."

"Why?" Anyone who knew Paul would have asked the same question. "Like I said, practical matters weren't high on Paul's list of priorities."

"Like I said, maybe his priorities changed," Serras ventured.

Della sober and Paul responsible. And both dead.

"You should be getting a call from Flint shortly."

"Is that what brought you down here today? To check me out, the merry ex-wife?" I pushed my coffee cup aside, folded my arms on the tabletop and hunched toward Serras. "Okay, you got me. The gig's up. I killed Paul and made it look like suicide so I could inherit a mass of credit card bills that probably rival the national debt."

Serras took a long swallow of Wild Turkey, waited for my protest to continue. This time his silent technique worked.

"Don't be fooled by Paul's high-end address and designer threads. It was all part of the image. He knew how to put on a good show." Right up to the end.

"Rumor is he learned from a master."

Beneath that chiseled countenance, Serras was curious. And human after all.

"Are you waiting for me to blush, Detective?"

He stood six foot two and solid male. "I'm waiting for a lot more than that, LeGrande."

He got several steps away before my ability to speak was restored. "Serras?"

He looked at me over his shoulder.

"What else did you find? In that lock box?"

"Go see Johnny Flint. Over Debrese's Meats, off Central."

It's all he would give me. Unless you counted the parting shot of his prime-time backside. Which I did.

JOHNNY FLINT'S OFFICE was at the opposite end of the spectrum from Michael Kingsley's uptown firm of cherry-paneled suites and associates with Roman numerals following their surnames. The steep wooden staircase was dank, dark and smelled of ground beef and pickled tongue. I smiled as I read the slightly askew gold-letter decals across the door in need of a paint job. Jonathan V. Flint IV & Associates. Della would have loved this guy.

I opened the door to an attempt at a waiting room consisting of a faux leather sofa, two plastic armless chairs and several outdated magazines on a wood grain cocktail table. The room was empty except for what I assumed was the "Associate"—an answering machine with an unlit message light.

Jonathan V. Flint IV appeared in a suit with a Teflon texture, moving toward me with both hands outstretched. "Ms. Chumsky, my condolences on your loss." He took both my hands in his and began levering my arms as if I were a pump on a well gone dry.

"Thank you for seeing me on such short no-

tice. And it's LeGrande," I corrected him, con-
tracting my biceps and halting his frenetic hello
on a downward swing. "What's the V for?"

He stepped back, still holding my hands as
he sized me up. He came up to my chin. I gave
him two points for not doing a comb over
where the white skin of his scalp shone. The
rest he would have to earn.

His smile was a little too oily. I deducted a
point.

"Some would say 'vampire.'"

"What am I going to say?"

"'Very glad to have made your acquaintance.'"

I wasn't completely convinced yet. "And
the 'IV?'"

"That stands for the fifth with a few ounces
missing that I always have in my file cabinet."
He winked at me. "Hidden from Mrs. Jonathan
V. Flint IV."

I smiled and let him lead me into his office,
still holding one of my hands.

"Please." He gestured with a generous flourish to one of the beige tweed chairs facing a
desktop messy with piles of papers. Johnny
Flint sat down on the opposite of the desk and
looked at me. I smiled, trying not to show sympathy, but we both knew it. Johnny Flint was

hanging on by a fancy nameplate and a few stacks of mostly blank pages.

Again the contrast between Flint and any number of lawyers Paul knew personally from the country club slapped me across the head. I sensed Paul had chosen Johnny Flint precisely because he was so far outside the sphere dominated by Michael Kingsley and the like. Why?

"Did you know my ex-husband personally, Mr. Flint, or just professionally?"

"Please call me 'Fourth.'" Flint grinned. So did I.

"Speaking of which—" he stood, moved toward the file cabinet and opened the top drawer, removing a bottle of scotch "—may I offer you a drink?"

"No, thank you." I didn't even have to snap my rubber band. Some days were like that. Good days. "But please, don't let me stop you."

"I had no intention of letting you," he said as he sat down and poured a generous measure into a coffee mug. We exchanged smiles again.

"Perhaps coffee?" Despite his shiny skull, his chin-level stature and his seedy surroundings, Flint had an inbred graciousness that made me wonder if the nameplate was more than a matter of public relations after all.

I glanced at the dark liquid in the yellowed

glass carafe, film floating over its still surface. Again I declined.

Flint propped his elbows, interlaced his fingers and gave me a thoughtful, sincere lawyerly look. "Your husband—"

"Ex-husband," I corrected. I gave him an equally sincere, thoughtful, former-woman-who'd-paid-the-bills-taking-off-her-clothes look.

Flint nodded, acknowledging his mistake. He steepled his fingers. I crossed my legs.

"Your ex-husband, Ms.—" He paused, not anxious to make another mistake.

"LeGrande. Silver LeGrande," I reminded softly.

"Your ex-husband, Ms. LeGrande," he began again, "came to me three months ago and hired me to prepare his will." Flint shuffled through the stacks of papers, inspected several manila folders, finally selecting one. "Ahh, here we are."

I smiled at him. Whatever Flint's shortcomings, he wasn't going down without a show. I thought of Paul and Della and stopped smiling.

"Prior to that, I'd never had the privilege of knowing Mr. Chumsky. Although I was pleased to make his acquaintance and honored to represent him."

"Paul retained you for other legal services."

"I was at his disposal but, unfortunately, our relationship was limited to the particular service of drawing up his last will and testament." Flint shook his head. "I was shocked to learn of his demise not long after."

"Quite a coincidence, wouldn't you say?" I could almost hear Auntie's disbelieving snort.

"As a lawyer, Ms. LeGrande—"

"If I can call you Fourth, you certainly should call me Silver."

"It would be my honor. As a lawyer, Silver—" his smile dissolved and his eyes turned shrewd "—I have learned to be careful what I do and don't say. Your ex-husband came to me to draw up a will. It's not exactly out of the ordinary."

"Unless a short time later you're found strung up like one of the sides of beef in your landlord's shop below."

Flint steepled his fingers again, tapped them against his thin lips.

"Paul must have mentioned to you he was the pro at the Meadows Country Club."

"I'm not a member, Silver, but I do like to hit the greens now and then with clients and was aware of your ex-husband's reputation at the Meadows."

"I don't mean to offend you, Fourth, but then surely you were aware in his line of work Paul made contacts with some of the more well-known law firms in the city."

"Yet he came to me." Flint concluded my point.

"Possibly if he'd met you outside the office?"

Flint shook his head.

"Or had been recommended to you by another client?"

Again Flint shook his head. "Silver," he began, adopting the soft tone of guidance I'd like to imagine my father might have used... had I ever known the bastard. "Having a simple will drawn up is not a complex task. Some people download a few templates, fill them out, sign them in front of a few friends, file them away and they're done with it. Of course, that's not the method I would recommend." He smiled beguilingly. "Perhaps your ex-husband saw no point in paying higher legal fees than he had to for a basic service."

I shook my head. "The day before his death, Paul had been seen leaving the apartment of a woman strangled the night before. When the police brought Paul in to ask a few questions about his relationship with the woman, Michael Kingsley had one of his key people down there before Paul could tell the cops to kiss his nine iron."

"He also left a message on my machine that night."

"What?" I looked at Flint in surprise.

"I shared a similar reaction, Silver. He called very late, actually very early if you are looking at it from the proper perspective. Around 2:30 a.m. I believe. He said he'd recently been interviewed by the police and he wanted to come in and see me the next day around noon. He did not sound exactly himself."

I knew Flint was being generous. Paul would have been snookered to his socks by that time.

"He never showed. Soon after, I learned of his unfortunate situation." He gave a respectful pause before continuing. "Maybe your ex-husband came to me precisely because I was so far out of the country club's select circle." Flint echoed my earlier musings. "Maybe he didn't feel comfortable with anyone he had a professional and/or personal contact with on a daily basis knowing his financial assets."

That made sense. "Razzle-dazzle 'em" was mandatory to Paul's success.

"On the other hand, Silver," Flint met my gaze, "lawyers who achieve the status of Michael Kingsley are in a very unique position.

They don't do anything unless there's something in it for them."

I considered Flint's words. "I was surprised to see a high-priced mouthpiece from Kingsley and Associates riding in to Paul's rescue, especially since the police had nothing and Paul probably knew it. On the other hand, Paul also probably wouldn't want to detract from his image by revealing his less-than-impressive financial holdings."

Flint frowned. He slid out a pair of wire frames from his inside breast jacket pocket and perched them halfway down his nose. He opened the manila folder with its neatly typed label, Chumsky, Paul, across its end tab. "On the contrary, Silver," he said in the same fatherly tone I was warming up to too fast. "Of course, its been a few months and circumstances might have altered since my last meeting with Mr. Chumsky, but—" He raised his gaze from the papers before him. "When the will was drawn up, your ex-husband had a respectable showing of assets."

Paul and *respectable*. No offense to my dearly departed ex-husband, but even he would admit the two words rarely found themselves together in the same sentence.

"Paul? Respectable?" I repeated aloud.

Flint's gaze dropped down to the papers before him. He nodded approvingly. "Quite."

"Define 'respectable,' Fourth."

His gaze came up over the wire rims. "A half-million dollars."

I was too stunned to speak, let alone swear.

"Give or take a few 'thou.'" Flint smiled. He was having fun now. He directed his gaze through the wire rims as he ran an index finger down a typed list before him. "Distributed over several accounts. I advised your ex-husband to look into tax-free munis or even consider real estate, which traditionally produces a strong return."

I snapped my rubber band once, twice, thrice. "When you say 'assets,' you mean the house, car, the whole enchilada." That made sense. Estimated property value of Paul's bungalow had to be "quite respectable," although Paul's prior practices would have had it mortgaged to the hilt.

Flint's gaze dropped again. "No, no. These are cash assets, in addition to the house and car."

This time I swore.

"Of course, any outstanding debts, monthly costs that accumulate, et cetera, will have to be paid until the estate is settled. And there's inheritance tax, my fees, miscellaneous costs, but then it's yours, Silver." Flint raised his gaze again over the wireless rims. "The whole enchilada."

After I learned Paul had made me executor of the will, I'd realized it was not so surprising. Paul had not been close with his family. His father had worked the oil rigs and had shared the same weaknesses as his son—liquor and women—only, he had been an ugly drunk and Paul had several capped teeth as testimony. His mother had died of ovarian cancer three years ago. I had gone back to Texas with him and held his hand. Paul's sister was a born—again revivalist that made Tammy Fay Baker look tasteful and had long ago given her big brother up to the Devil.

"As executor, you will be responsible for the funeral arrangements."

I nodded, surprised to find the simple movement required a Herculean effort. Executor, I could understand. Even sole inheritor I could reason away with some effort. But a half-million dollars in cash was going to demand explanation. A numbness from the past few days seeped into me. My muscles seemed wobbly, my thoughts disjointed.

"Perhaps I will have that cup of coffee after all, Fourth."

"Of course." The lawyer got up, checked a cup to make sure it was clean and filled it.

"Sweet and light," I said.

"As all things should be," he said as he handed me the cup with a kind smile.

I smiled back gratefully, wrapped both hands around the mug and lifted it to my lips. The lukewarm liquid tasted oily and bitter. I didn't care. I took a large swallow, caffeine the only legal pleasure I had left at the moment.

I set down the cup, extended Flint another grateful smile. "When Paul came to see you, did he indicate any reason why he'd decided to draw up a will?"

Flint tipped his head back, directed his gaze to the cheaply framed print on the wall behind me. "Illness? Maybe a recent accident had scared him or the death of someone he knew? Someone around the same age as he?"

I leaned in, propping an elbow on my knee and my chin on my fist. "Maybe he was afraid of someone? Someone who might want to do him harm?"

Flint's gaze came back to me, curious. "You think someone murdered your husband?"

"Ex-husband." I set the record straight. "I was with Paul the night before he...before I saw him the next morning..." I euphemized.

"You found him?"

I nodded.

"Poor dear," he said with such parental sympathy, I wondered if Flint had children and if not, would he like to adopt an overgrown former tassel twirler?

"So you were one of the last people to see him alive?"

"Yes. And if he was depressed, he wasn't showing it. Sure, he was drinking heavily, but it would have been more unusual if he hadn't. Then I really would have known something was wrong. It just seems to me, Fourth," I appealed earnestly, "there would have been a sign."

"You would think rightly so," Flint agreed. He took a large swallow from his coffee mug, his expression pensive as he swallowed and waited for the splashdown in his gut. "I assumed he wanted the will to protect his recently acquired financial good fortune."

"Hardly the kind of dough you'd accumulate on a country club pro's salary. Did he talk about it?"

"He said he had a windfall, bit of a lucky run."

"That's it?"

"He didn't volunteer more. I didn't ask."

I let out a long sigh. "And you didn't see him again?"

"He came in to sign the will once it was completed. He took a copy, asked me to keep the original, said it was easier that way. He had a habit of misplacing things." He paused for a quick, kind smile. "Said if anything should happen to him that I should contact you immediately. Except for that phone call, I didn't have contact with him again."

I set the coffee cup on the desk corner, gathered my purse, uncrossed my legs. "Well, thank you, Fourth. I appreciate your time." I stood.

"It should not be a complicated matter to settle the estate." Flint folded his glasses, slipped them into his coat pocket as he stood. "In the interim, if you'd like someone to oversee the deceased's affairs, it's a service I often provide for my clients for a nominal fee. Of course, any financial transactions, selling of property, payment of bills, investments, for example, would be initiated and approved by you."

"I'll keep that in mind." I plucked one of his business cards from the brass-plated holder on the desk. "I'll call you after the funeral is taken care of." I wondered if Paul's body had been released from the M.E.'s office yet.

"Oh, yes, about the funeral. I almost forgot."

Flint fumbled for his glasses again, perched them on his nose and shuffled through the papers. "Your ex-husband mentioned something about that. Now where is it?"

"Paul left instructions concerning his funeral arrangements?" Again, decidedly not a Paul Chumsky characteristic. The idea of death—especially his own–made Paul squirm. He was a man who, until the other night had successfully avoided life's grimmer realities at all costs.

"Not instructions, mind you, but he did make a comment that he asked me to convey to you should something...well, no need to go there again. Ah! Here it is." Flint's index finger stopped halfway down a page. "He said concerning the funeral, you should confer with Billic." Flint looked up from the paper. "She would know his wishes."

"What the hell does that mean?"

Flint slid off his glasses, folded them, looked at me with that sage, fatherly expression that made me want to trust him. "I believe you will have to ask Billie."

Chapter Six

I went to see Serras. I caught him heading toward the departmental parking lot across the street from the station. I parked illegally, shouted, "Hey!" as I bounded out of my car. I weaved through the other vehicles and faced him across the front end of a Chevy Caprice. Before he even parted his lips, I held up my hand to silence him. He tilted his head, gave me the long, slow look. I slammed my hand down on the hot metal hood. My palm smarted. It felt damn delicious.

"You knew." I rounded the hood, the burn in my hand little consolation for the mounting confusion and fury inside me. "You knew."

He watched my approach with his cop's coolness that could have easily sent me over the edge. I poked my index finger into his chest, determined to elicit some kind of emotion. "Even before I went there, you'd seen the bank accounts. You knew."

Serras stared down at my finger in the middle of his chest as if it were an alien life form. His gaze came up, returned to mine.

"I'm a detective, LeGrande. It's my business to know."

"You sent me over to Johnny Flint without a clue. You set me up."

"I'd say that was the work of your ex-husband." He gently pushed my finger off his chest, moved to the driver's door, opened it and got in. I stamped over, pounded on the window. It lowered.

"What's that mean? I'm a suspect? Because my ex-husband left me some money?"

Serras swung his head from side to side as if relieving tension in his neck. "No, Silver, you're not a suspect."

"Why not?"

He shot me an ill-tempered look. "Because the case is closed."

The Caprice rolled into reverse, the driver's window smoothly sealing. I stood there until it took the corner and disappeared. I should have stuck Serras with the silverware when I had the chance.

Billie was in the storage room, checking inventory when I arrived at the club. I called her name at the room's entrance so as not to startle her.

She turned, no surprise in her face as if she'd been expecting me, and set down the clipboard.

"They closed Paul's case."

She showed no reaction. Of course she knew, probably before Serras did. Now she watched me, the harsh overhead light making no friends with her face. She set down her clipboard. "What did you expect, Silver?"

"Good question." I sighed. "Exactly what happened."

"The medical examiner says death by asphyxiation by strangulation. No one else was there, nothing gone, no signs of struggle. Paul was very drunk—but if it wasn't suicide, he would have fought back."

"Not if he was enjoying it," I pointed out. "And someone pulled the chair out from under him."

Billie gave me an indulgent smile, humoring me. She picked up her clipboard. "Come on out to the dining room. I'll have Sweet Sam bring us beignets and coffee." She linked my arm through hers, patted my knuckles. "Did you see my handsome Lexi?"

"Yes," I said without enthusiasm.

"And he told you the coroner's office had ruled Paul's death a suicide?"

"Actually all I got out of him was the case was closed."

"Do you know the story they tell about Lexi?" She did not wait for my answer. Her hand stayed warm on mine. "He was working vice. He was young but he was Royce's boy, and his dad had died in the line of fire. They partnered him with an old crew cut, no—neck, Jimmy 'Mad Dog' Barnes. One night they get a tip on a dealer moving a lot of heroin. They go to the dealer's place to bust him but all they find is a Saturday-night special and a key to a storage shed rented by the month. Mad Dog pockets them both. They hustle the dealer into the back seat, his cooperation their word against his, and they take a ride. Mad Dog tells Lexi to sit tight with the dealer. He'll go in and check it out. He comes back, tells Lexi the storage shed is empty. It's late. Nobody's around. Mad Dog puts the car in gear as if to take the dealer home, but Lexi sees him check out the street, take his hand off the wheel, reach in his pocket for the dealer's gun. Lexi aimed for Mad Dog's arm and pulled the trigger as Mad Dog pulled out the Saturday-night special and pointed it straight at Lexi's head. But Mad Dog ducked and took the bullet in the temple. Lexi grabs the dealer, takes him with him to the storage shed and grabs the bag inside. He drives Mad Dog and the dealer to the station, drags the dealer into Ealy's office, dumps the bag on his desk, tells him Mad Dog's out in the car with his brains blown out."

"What was in the bag?" I asked.

"Over a million dollars." She patted my hand once more before she released it. "Homicide may have closed the case but that doesn't mean it's over."

We entered the main room, and Billie called to a black man filling the wall cooler. "Sweet Sam, can I trouble you to make one of your famous pots of coffee and warm a few beignets for me and our favorite girl here."

Sweet Sam's face broke into a wide toothless smile as he moved toward us. He was a giant of a man, as if God had given him increased physical attributes to compensate for his limited mental development. Like most men his size, he had a gentleness belying his strength. His nature was childlike and generous. He didn't know his parents or much about his past. Billie had found him out back over a decade ago, digging in the garbage bin, and he'd been with her ever since.

"Miss Silver. You come back to me and Miss Billie."

"As if I could stay away." I met Sweet Sam as he rounded the bar. My feet lifted off the floor as he gave me a hug. I heard my ribs crunch. My own arms would not reach around his middle.

"How you been, darlin'?" I kissed his unlined cheek.

"I good, Miss Silver."

"You're not letting Miss Billie work you too hard?"

The large man smiled. "Not Sweet Sam."

"Good."

"Sam, put Silver down now."

He dropped me. My feet hit the floor.

"I get coffee, right, Miss Billie?"

Billie nodded. "Thank you, Sam."

He flashed me a final smile and moved toward the kitchen. Billie had sat down at her table and was waiting for me.

I sat down opposite her. "I didn't see him yesterday at Della's funeral."

"I gave him the day off. He doesn't understand death."

"Amen," I said.

"I didn't want him to hear the talk, see the tears. It upsets him."

I nodded understanding. "Goodness, he's got some gray hair. Never thought of him as getting old."

Billie screwed a cigarette into a rhinestone

holder. "Only physically. With his simple perspective, he'll probably outlive us all."

I looked in the direction of the kitchen. "We should all be so smart as Sweet Sam."

Billie gestured with the cigarette in its jeweled baton. She didn't light it. She rarely smoked. The cigarette and its holder were a prop. She enjoyed the look. "I worry what will become of him if something should happen to me." She rested the tip of the cigarette holder lightly between her lips.

"Are you worried something will happen to you?"

She waved the cigarette holder. "Recent events have made me a bit morbid, I suppose."

"Do you have a will?"

Her gaze that had blurred with contemplation of life's mysteries came back into sharp focus. "Should I?"

"Paul did."

If she was surprised, she didn't show it. Sweet Sam came out the kitchen door carrying a tray, which he set down on the table.

"Thank you, Sam. I'll serve." All the time Billie's gaze stayed on me. She set the cigarette and its holder in a clean ashtray. She poured the dark coffee, handed me a cup. She didn't speak until Sweet Sam had retreated into the kitchen. "You sound surprised."

I stirred in several sugars, cream. "You don't."

She offered me the plate of warm pastries, set them down, picked up the cigarette holder and sucked in lightly. "It's not what I would expect, but then, what is?" The cigarette holder made a low whistling noise as she drew in once morc.

I reviewed the last few days. Billie had a point. I peeled a top layer off the warm roll. "That's only the beginning." I rolled the layer, pulled it into two halves, then quarters, picked up a piece and gradually brought it to my lips. A stripper knows the pace of seduction. Slow. Billie languidly stirred her own coffee, gave me a patient smile. I was not teaching her anything she hadn't learned at Lottic the Body's knee.

We sipped, took dainty bites and chewed, two civilized chicks in Tennessee's most infamous strip club about to discuss murder.

I patted my lips with a napkin, folded it, set it beside the china plate. I looked around the room lush with velvet and brocade and gleaming wood. For the first time I could remember, I did not feel safe here. "Paul also left me his estate."

Billie's teeth, clamped on the cigarette holder, showed. "Was he going for the last laugh?"

"Without a doubt." I took a sip of coffee. "He left me over a half-million dollars."

Billie muttered what I loosely translated as the Cajun French equivalent of 'jumping Jehosephat.' A deep breath later, she had composed herself into her usual island of calm and regal bearing. "I had no idea country club pros do so well."

"They don't."

"So you were stunned?"

"Shell-shocked down to my Victoria's Secret."

"You must invest it wisely. I will give you some names. Blue-chip."

"I'd like to know where the money came from before I start amassing dividends."

Billie ran her thumb and forefinger up and down the sleek length of the cigarette holder, gave me an oblique glance. "You look a gift horse in the mouth, *chère?*"

"Della was murdered, Billie. Paul was, too."

Billie's brows lifted. "You are a detective now?"

Billie was asking questions. Avoiding answers. An immeasurable sadness hit me. It was not the first time that week. I dryly swallowed.

"I'll be making the funeral arrangements, of course."

Billie made a tsking sound, swung her large, handsome head slowly. "Too many funerals." She leveled her gaze on mine. "No more."

It was a warning.

"You bury your ex-husband. You invest your money wisely. You will have a good life."

"Life's more than a moderate portfolio, Billie."

On Billie's face, I saw the sadness that had jellied my own bones. "You don't know what you're getting into, *chère*."

"Same as Della?"

She delicately bit into a pastry.

"Same as Paul?"

The sadness stayed on her face, filled her black eyes as she looked at me. "Let the police handle this."

She meant Scrras. That was why she'd told me the story. He was a clean cop. A cop that could be trusted. A man to whom the official word meant squat.

"Paul also passed on a request to his lawyer concerning his funeral."

One eyebrow arched as Billie placidly chewed.

"How did the lawyer put it…concerning the

funeral arrangements, Paul said I should confer with you. You would know his wishes."

Billie's fist came down hard on the table, rattling china. Coffee sloshed out of my cup. Billie's head dropped back and laughter rumbled from the excessive depths of her. "That bastard. That bastard." She wiped the mascara away from beneath her eyes. "He got the last laugh after all."

"What's going on, Billie? Tell me."

She shook her head resolutely. "No. No. I'll have no more blood on my hands."

"Why did Paul say come to you, you would know his wishes? Where did he get over a half-million dollars? And he didn't kill himself, did he?" It was my turn to slap the table. Both palms. The table barely quivered.

Billie's soft hand covered mine again, gripped it too tight as if she'd already lost me. Her voice took on a gentle lilt. "Della and Paul are dead, Silver. You pursue this and you'll die, too."

"How do you know that?"

"Because I told them the exact same thing. And your ex-husband—" Billie's eyes suddenly filled with tears. Unashamed she let them slide down her smooth cheeks, but her voice was steady. "Did I ever tell you how much I liked your husband?"

I didn't even correct the term to ex-husband. I was going marshmallow myself.

"He had his qualities."

Billie gestured to Sweet Sam, who had come out but stayed his distance at the far end of the long bar, dusting bottles. "Sweet Sam, love, bring me a glass and a bottle of whiskey. The good stuff."

Hell, it was turning into an Irish wake. I waited while Billie poured and downed a shot in one smooth motion. She did not offer me one. God bless her. Because for the first time in forty-nine months, I might have said yes.

"Paul did it for the money but he did it to help Della, too." She downed another shot. I hoped for revelation.

"The man had his faults, but the most pain he caused was to himself."

"You weren't married to him." But I smiled to show I agreed with her.

Another shot. I worried Billie was going maudlin on me. Which was not like her at all. She could drink any man her size or smaller under the table and not get sappy.

"Why did they die, Billie?"

Her gaze took me in and spit me out. "Because they did not listen to me. I warned them." She poured a whiskey but slowed to a sip, eyeing me over the glass. "Paul had told me to wear red, serve Cajun shrimp and dance at his funeral." She leaned in, her voice a low dirge. "I will not dance, *chère*."

She brought the glass to her lips. "That's why he told you to come see me, I would know what he wants for his funeral. He knew if anything happened to him and you got any foolish, romantic notions—"

I shot her a withering gaze.

"I would warn you."

"Consider me warned." The coffee was cold. I finished it anyway. "Now tell me why."

She pushed back from the table and hoisted her ample body. I wasn't getting another thing out of her. She left the glass but took the whiskey bottle. She laid her hand on my shoulder, pressed down with unnecessary pressure. "I will not dance at your funeral, either, Silver."

I decided not to broach the subject of serving Cajun shrimp.

ADRIENNE AND AUNTIE were sunbathing topless in the backyard when I got home. I rifled through the pile of mail on the counter, stopped at an envelope addressed to me. The return address was the college. I sat down, slit open the envelope. I had been placed on academic probation.

Adrienne and Auntie came in looking like my ghosts of Christmas past and future. "Hey Silverado." Adrienne opened the refrigerator. Perkiness reached new heights. "What's shaking?"

I threw the letter onto the table. Auntie sat down. "Part of the Academic Early Intervention System," Adrienne read over her shoulder. They both looked up at me.

"And that, ladies, is the best news I've gotten all day."

Adrienne sat down beside Auntie. They propped their breasts on their folded arms, their expressions grave. "Actually this is not as bad as it looks, Silver," Adrienne began. "It's a mechanism put into place to identify students experiencing problems before it's too late to overcome their difficulties."

Auntie nodded sagely. I began to giggle. Auntie and Adrienne exchanged looks.

"I'm sorry," I said, wiping away tears. "Take it from an old stripper. If you two want to be taken seriously, you have to at least put on pasties."

I expected at least a blush from Adrienne. Nothing. Auntie was doing all right by her.

"Quit stalling," Auntie demanded. "What's going on?"

I recounted my day.

"What are you going to do?" Adrienne asked.

I pushed back my chair, got up and went to the cupboard. "I'm going to make a praline cheesecake."

MONDAY MORNING I learned Paul's body had been released from the morgue. The funeral was set for Wednesday. Monday night I had a gig. A chiropractic convention was going on in town and one of the larger medical equipment companies had hired out Luxury Limos for the night. Ten men with receding hairlines and swelling waistlines piled into the limo like a pack of eager prom kings. Their energy was high and their comments to me typical of a middle-aged man when confronted with a five-foot-eleven, red-haired limo driver in fishnets, stilettos and a top hat. Luxury Limousines hadn't hired me for my U-turns.

The champagne was already pouring, fizz that I'd be scratching dry off the back seat at 4:00 a.m. It was going to be a long night of sirloin, booze and exotic dancers, and at the end of the run, my wallet swelling with twenties. I put the limo into Drive and headed toward Beale Street without even asking.

The boys were inside a high-end restaurant, chewing rare beef and throwing back Sambuca shots. I was parked at the corner a block over, leaning against the front hood, sucking a Tootsie Pop. Several tourists asked to take their picture with me. Billie's marquee was in the distance along with the offer of voodoo protection from Mary the Wonder. The Monarch, known as the Castle of Missing Men since its gunshot victims and dead gamblers could be easily disposed at the undertaker's place that had shared the back alley, was long gone along with the red-light district one block over on Gayoso that had rivaled New Orleans' Storyville. The Beale Street Management Corporation had taken over the redevelopment of Beale Street in the late seventies, and downtown Memphis was reborn.

I chewed the pop's center, then on the bare stick, considered the chapters in the textbook on the front seat I had to read before Monday, wondered who killed Della and Paul and why? The waiting around was the worst part of an all-night run but you couldn't leave a thirty-foot white stretch with high tires alone. I was contemplating having another Tootsie Pop when I saw Serras moving toward me. He'd obviously spotted me first. In stilettos and black satin hot pants, leaning against a thirty-foot lady, I wasn't hard to miss.

"Silver." He moved into my personal space.

I crossed my arms. "Serras," I said through my teeth.

He gave me a good once-over. "Not many women could pull that off." His gaze came back to mine. The man had a heat that could part a Baptist's thighs. I decided to have that Tootsie Pop. I offered the bag to Serras. He took a red one.

"You on the clock, Serras?" I asked, the lollipop stick shooting out of my mouth's corner, and my body language hanging tough.

"I'm always on the clock." He unwrapped the Tootsie, popped it into his mouth, taking in everything around him, although his gaze never left mine.

"Yeah, well, what are you hanging around me for? I'm parked legally. Maybe you need me to identify another victim the department is going to ignore?"

"Just a friendly howdy-do."

"I have all the friends I need."

He feigned disappointment. "I'm sensing an angry undercurrent."

I gave him a dry look. "When my friends get murdered and the police write it off, I tend to get touchy."

He pulled the Tootsie out of his mouth, making a popping sound. "Could be hormonal."

I cocked a hip. "You got a wife, Serras?"

"Not anymore."

"Probably because you talked to her like that."

"Nah, she fell in love with my first partner. Even got him to quit the force, open a security consulting firm. They got three kids and a four-bedroom, two-and-a-half bath in the burbs."

Why the hell did he have to go and do that? Share a piece of his past, make me realize he was as vulnerable as any schmoo.

"I'm sorry." I was loath to do it, but I let him glimpse my sensitive side.

"Don't be." He smiled, chewing on his lollipop stick. "She's a hell of a lot better off than with me."

God bless him. If he'd been anyone else, I would have planted a big wet one on him right there. That worried me. "You're not trying to make me like you, are you, Serras?"

"Not particularly."

"Must be a slow night for crime, then."

"Never a slow night."

I crunched, cracking the candy coating. The sugar rush got my synapses jumping. I smiled. "You're feeling guilty. You know whoever murdered Paul and Della is still out there and it's eating at you."

He rolled the lollipop in his mouth, shifting the stick to the opposite corner.

"Billie said if the decision was made to close the case, it was not made by you. She seems to be a big fan of yours."

"You've been visiting with Billie. What else did she have to say?"

"She said you shot a dirty cop in the face."

Not even a muscle twitched. I'd heard the expression cold, blue steel. Now I'd seen it. I waited but when he gave me no response, I said, "She also thinks I should invest my money wisely, enjoy my life and let this business go."

"Good advice. Are you going to follow it?"

"The money's not clean, Serras. I don't know where it came from but I intend to find out. What about you? If history proves right, you don't seem the type to let someone get away with murder."

He switched the stick to the other side of his mouth. "What I'm going to do is not the issue."

I narrowed my gaze. Another sugar-induced insight shot to my brain. "Billie sent you, didn't she? Damn. She's worried about me and asked you to keep an eye out."

My party with their bellies full of beef and

their heads full of booze spilled out of the restaurant, primed to continue their night crawling.

Serras lifted a brow as they beelined for the limo. "Looks like the gang's all here."

I angled my top hat. "Gal's gotta a make living, Serras."

"Not when she inherited a half mil."

I eyeballed him. "Doesn't that give you pause? A country club pro with a fat bank account?"

"It's a country club pro's ex-wife with a fat bank account now."

"Either way, it's enough to make me curious."

"C'mon sweetheart," one of my lovelies called once they were all safely packed in. I already heard the slur in his voice.

Serras yanked open the door, leaned into the limo so his suit jacket fell open and his shield caught the streetlight. "Your driver will be with you in one minute, gentlemen." He closed the door.

"Why, you're a regular charmer when push comes to shove." I smiled to show him I liked it. "But I better go before the boys get restless."

He wrapped his fingers around my forearm, stopping me. I looked down at his hand, back up at him. "Okay, you've got my attention, Detective."

"I have a feeling you're in for a long night. While you're waiting for these bazookas to be done with their carousing, think. Think about that last night with your ex-husband. Maybe he said something, hinted, anything about what he and Della Devine were in on."

"I thought the case was closed."

"Officially, yes."

I smiled, leaned over and planted that big wet one on his lips. "God bless you, Serras," I whispered, surprising us both.

Chapter Seven

I deposited the boys a few blocks over at Billie's and told them to behave themselves. I was voicing notes from my text into my portable tape recorder on rising interest rates which lead to reduced investment spending, not understanding a damn thing I was saying when the boys filed out of the club. I could see by their faces they'd decided it was time to get a little less civilized. Billie's was for tourists and curiosity seekers. These boys were ready for hardcore carousing. I steered the limo in the direction of the Oyster Club. The limo was sweet with liquor, smoke and raw language. I lowered the divider to show I was a sport.

I parked in a side alley near the Oyster. The boys tumbled out with an impressive zeal considering the hour and the amount of liquor they'd consumed. I pointed them in the right direction and promised to stay local. I heard the swell of music and catcalls as the doors opened, my boys pausing for a sobering moment before a six-foot-six burly bouncer with skin the color of night. He looked past them. I recognized Big Man Mooney. It was a small, small, strip-club world after all. I gave the massive man a jaunty wave and tipped my top hat. He flashed white teeth. "Silver, you gorgeous thing, these fellas belong to you?"

I showed my palms in surrender. "Who else, Mooney? Send my kickback care of Luxury Limos."

The boys were chomping at the bit, sneaking peeks past Mooney's wide form. Mooney waved them inside with a courtly flourish, watched me appreciatively as I came over to the club door.

"Damn, girl."

My hips involuntarily shimmied. What can I say? You can take the girl off the stage but you can't take the stage out of the girl.

"You can't be telling me you left Billie's to shuttlebus sorry butts like those around for quick rounds of touch and tickle."

"Pretty cocky coming from an Oyster Club maitre d'," I countered. "When did you go legit?" Mooney had been a strong arm for Vito Figuero, who controlled the city's underworld.

Figuero and his men had been frequent customers at Billie's although Billie never permitted them to do any business inside her club. Figuero had respected that.

"Just filling in, doing a little favor for an old friend of Mr. Figuero's." Mooney's teeth gleamed white in the neon glow. His head was completely shaved, his skull so smooth and dark and powerfully shaped, I wanted to rub it and make a wish.

"Mr. Figuero has an investment here?" I speculated. "And business is down a bit?"

Mooney kept smiling, the neon giving his teeth a green cast. "I don't keep the books."

"But strangled strippers. They do have a way of putting a damper on the festivities."

Mooney offered me a cigarette. I shook my head. He clamped one between his lips, struck a match against the side of the building. He drew in, exhaled, squinted at me through the smoke. "I'd seen her on Billie's stage." He nodded, taking a long drag. "She was really something."

For an eulogy, it wasn't bad. "You ever see her here?"

"Yeah, once in a while when I have business in the neighborhood, I'd stop in here."

"Check on Mr. Figuero's investments?"

"Cute." He chucked me under the chin. It wasn't exactly a benign gesture. "She was cute, too. Used to hit me up for smokes. Told me she was quitting. Told me I should, too." He took one more drag, flicked the cigarette. "She was right. Should quit. Damn things are going to kill me."

"Who killed her, Mooney?"

He gave me a knockdown stare. I couldn't tell if he was insulted or impressed. He spit a piece of tobacco off his tongue. "Read the papers."

"I did."

Mooney shrugged his shoulders the size of cantaloupes. "Not the first time a man found his woman spreading her legs for someone else and lost his mind." He leaned toward me. "Love," he said with a Motown smoothness. "Makes a man do crazy things."

I had expected the song and dance from Mooney. He'd been Figuero's boy for too long. "So who was the other man Della was seeing?" *Convince me,* my question told him.

He shot me an irritated look as he left to attend to two guys swaggering toward the door. He came back, arms crossed, his biceps thick and meaty as quartered beef and his mood definitely no longer touchy-feely.

"She was twenty-seven, Mooney. She was my friend. And the guy they say killed her, then hung himself. That 'jealous lover'—he was my ex-husband."

He shook his beautifully carved head. "Sorry to hear that, Silver," he said with such surprising sincerity I was tempted to believe him. I saw his muscles tighten and knew that was all I'd get out of him.

"What's your boss think of that?" I cocked my head toward the complex's towers rising like phoenixes above the east side.

Mooney lit another cigarette, expelled the smoke through the gap between his front teeth. Mr. Figuero's a businessman. He embraces progress."

In other words, he got in on the ground floor, I thought.

"Mooney," a woman's voice growled just inside the entry. "Last call's coming. Come on in before someone gets ugly."

Mooney held out his hands. "Duty calls, my darling."

"Do me a favor and send my fellas out in one piece?" I patted his solid chest. The man could have been a rock-climbing wall for pygmics.

He gave me a small salute. I let him watch me as I walked back to the limo. I was opening the door, airing out the smells of debauchery when I saw Lucy hurry out from behind the building, puffing hard and fast on a cigarette, her heels clicking on the cement. She turned toward me and stopped dead, staring at the limo, then at me. The hard lines of her face faded as surprise rounded her eyes. What I wouldn't have given to open the back door and have Tall, Dark and Handsome step out, brandishing a bouquet of roses.

Lucy stuck her cigarette in her mouth, sucked hard and snapped out of it. So did I. She moved toward me, taking it all in with every step.

"Don't ask," I warned with a smile to show I wasn't the enemy.

She cracked a grin, expelled a stream of smoke. "I wasn't going to say a word."

I hadn't seen her at the funeral and had been strangely disappointed. "Did you hear they closed the case?" I watched her reaction. The cigarette dangled from the corner of her mouth, its filter red-lipstick rimmed.

"Yeah?" She challenged. The cigarette bobbed up and down with a life of its own. I watched fascinated, waiting for it to fall. Lucy's lips tightened around it. She inhaled, exhaled out the other side of her mouth. She never touched the cigarette once. It was a damn parlor trick.

"Heard her boyfriend did her, then got senti-mental about it and strung himself up." The cig-arette jerked up, down, underscoring each sordid fact. "Also heard the fool was your ex-husband." The cigarette angled toward heaven as she emitted a low whistle. I was completely impressed.

"Except that call Della made. The one you overheard? When she was making plans to meet someone? She wasn't talking to my ex-hus-band. She was making plans to meet someone else."

Lucy chewed on her cigarette and looked bored. "So? Your ex-husband learns about this other guy, goes ballistic and did Della. He probably didn't even realize what he did until it was over."

The calico cat I'd seen on my first visit to the club slinked out from the alley, wound itself around Lucy's legs.

I shook my head. "They were friends. You know, hung out together, had a few laughs, kept each other company. They weren't in love with each other."

"Is that what he told you?" Lucy sent me a pitying look. "Is that why you're hanging around outside the club like some male fantasy?"

"No, really—" I saw my boys coming out,

beelining it toward the limo. I didn't have much time. "Do you have any idea who she could have been talking to that night?"

She parted her lips. The cigarette tumbled out, hit the sidewalk in a shower of sparks. The cat leaped away. Lucy ground the cigarette butt out with her heel. "I got to get home to my kids."

I didn't even bother to give her my number again. "You want a ride?"

She was surprised again.

"You can ride up front with me. What's coming toward us is about as close as I've got to Prince Charming, but it beats walking."

She studied me as if determining my motive. I heard my fares closing in. "They'll hoot and holler a bit but they'll be passed out not long after I pull away from the curb." I opened the front passenger door. "Wait a minute," I said, stacking the tape recorder on top of the text I'd left on the front seat and putting them inside the console. She hesitated before she slid inside. She glanced up at me as I started to close the door. I wasn't sure but I thought I heard her say, 'Thanks.'

I drove Lucy the long way to a seedy neighborhood, wishing someone besides crack heads could see her glide up to her door in a white stretch. I gave her the full treatment, jumping out of the car and rounding the front. She was snapping her purse closed as I opened the door. She slipped out.

"That call Della made…"

She did not meet my gaze. I waited, suppressing an excited "Yeah?"

"The cell phone she used. I saw it in the garbage. After she made the call, she threw it away."

"It stopped working?"

Her expression became long-suffering. "No."

She was going to make me work for this one. I thought. Slowly understanding dawned.

"So there would be no record of the call?"

"I gotta go. It's late." She headed toward the building.

Bingo. It was my turn to say thanks.

I took the boys back to their hotel, accepted their gratitude and was not disappointed. I drove back to Luxury Limos, parking the white stretch besides others in the dark parking lot. I spot-cleaned and aired out the car, gathered my textbook, tape recorder and purse and dropped the keys in a narrow slot in the office's back door.

I headed toward my car parked out of sight on a side street next to the building and contemplated stopping in an all-night diner on the way home. I always sleep better on a full stomach. I pressed automatic entry twice, heard the doors click unlocked. I opened the driver's door, threw my keys and purse on the front seat, reached to open the rear door to dump my text and tape recorder when I was jerked back and upward against a large, solid mass, my body dangling from a thin cord around my throat.

My arms flailed. My legs kicked out. The noose around my neck tightened. I couldn't breathe. My brain seemed to swell. My eyes bulged but things were going black. I clawed at the cord around my neck getting tighter, taking oxygen.

I whipped my head back and forth, the dangling silver shoulder-length earrings I'd borrowed from Auntie slapping me across the face. The pressure cutting into my neck increased.

"Where is it, bitch?"

"What?" I squeezed out with what seemed my last bit of breath.

"Don't play with me or you'll be joining your friends."

I tried to place the voice, but my brain was beginning to shut down.

"Where is it?"

What? I said inside my head, speech and oxygen cut off, a darkness moving in, tunneling my vision. The noose tightened. I felt the pointed tips of the earrings skim against my shoulders. Mustering any bit of air left, I tried to say, "I know." All that came out was a gasped, "I—"

"What?" The man leaned in.

Now. With a subhuman surge of strength, I yanked out the earrings and jabbed backward, aiming for an eyeball. I made contact. A surprised yelp, the release around my neck. Bingo. I fell to my knees, gasping, scrambled blindly into the front seat, searching for my keys. I locked the doors, sucking in great gulps of oxygen, trying to get my brain to clear and my vision to focus. I jammed the keys into the ignition, roared the motor to life, the dark colored dots swimming before me beginning to part. I threw my car into reverse, my vision only marred by random black dots and hazy haloes. I pressed the accelerator to the floor and shot backward out of the alley. I felt a bump, glanced in my rearview mirror, saw my $142.97 textbook flat as Pamela Anderson without modern medicine.

My attacker had recovered quicker than I. By the time I hit the lot, swerving around the limos, he was pulling out of the lot in a silver

minivan, the kind favored by suburban fami-
lies. He took a hard right, ran the light at the
intersection and was an easy half mile ahead of
me by the time I had him in my sights again.
Still the streets were empty, and I had a V-six
and a righteous rage. He took a corner, curv-
ing wide, before I could catch his license number. I punched the gas pedal to the floor,
reaching over to pop open the glove compartment, pulled out my .32. It had been a present
from my mother. I was almost to the corner
when I saw the police cruiser coming down
the opposite side of the street. Not having time
to brake, I went for broke, took the corner on
two wheels and said a prayer to my God, who
I'd always envisioned as a cross between
Mother Theresa and Mae West. I'd turned onto
a cross-town street with intersecting roads at
every block. The van was nowhere in sight.
The cruiser's flashing lights were framed in
my rearview mirror like a Coney Island ride. I
slowed, pulled over to the curb and stopped,
made sure the gun was in plain sight on the seat
next to me. I was banging my forehead against
the steering wheel when the cop tapped on my
window.

I was in the full throes of an indignant lather
by the time I lowered the window. "Fine thing.

You showing up now. Where were you ten minutes ago when I was being throttled by some lunatic in a silver soccer-mom mobile?"

"Ma'am—" The cop looked a rookie and was trying unsuccessfully to conceal his surprise. He moved his hand to rest on his gun. I couldn't say I blamed him.

"Is that a gun?"

"Or am I just happy to see you?" I couldn't resist.

"Get out of the car. Slowly."

"It's legit. It's registered and I have a permit," I told him. I slid out of the car, catching in the side mirrors the fresh welt circling my throat and the red pinpricks of blood marring the whites of my eyes. I straightened, a fishnetted, hot-panted, full five-eleven. "Listen," I held my palms out appealingly, saw his muscles tense as if readying to go for his gun again. "I know this doesn't look encouraging but I'm one of the good guys. Really."

He gave me a good once-over as he reached in for the .32. He didn't look convinced and suddenly not so young after all. He hefted the handgun in the palm of his hand. It was a small semiautomatic, almost delicate looking with its mother-of-pearl handle. No standard-issue

Glock but it could do the trick. "Do you know why I pulled you over?"

My first response was "You were lonely." I bit my tongue. Serras might be able to handle repartee but this flatfoot did not look so easy to amuse.

"You were going eighty in a forty mile zone."

"I can explain that." I shifted my body into a conversational pose. "You see—"

"License and registration."

Definitely a hard nut to crack. I decided to do it his way. "My license is in my wallet in my purse. My registration is in the glove compartment." We both stepped toward the car at the same time. I directed a pointed look at the hand he still rested on his holster. "Shall I get them?"

His eyes narrowed into an attempt at a mean squint. "I'll get them. He leaned into the car, over the driver's seat, popped open the glove compartment.

"Damn." I slapped my forehead as the cop straightened. "I should have shot out his tires."

Maybe it was my sincere self-disgust or maybe the cop was as weary as me. Either way, with one hand on his gun and the other wrapped around mine, he abandoned the formalities to finally ask, "Ma'am, what the hell are you talking about?"

I began with Della Devine dead in the morgue, speaking with an anxiety rate high enough to discourage interruption even from a man with a gun in either hand. When I ended, he waited, testing the waters to see if I was finally finished.

I was.

He rubbed his lantern jaw. "Ma'am, if you made that all up to get out of a ticket, I'd have to let you go on effort alone."

I opened my mouth to protest but he held up a hand. "However, I know the case. Even more so now," he added dryly. "I may regret doing this—" his smile was equally dry "—but I'll need to ask you a few questions about your attack. First, I'll radio in the description of the silver minivan and confirm you're the legally registered owner of this weapon."

"Of course," I agreed with amazing graciousness for a bleary-eyed, recently strangled limo driver in drag.

"If you'll have a seat in the back of the police car," he suggested with equal aplomb. I half waited for him to offer his arm. He pointed the direction with my gun. Close enough, I decided.

I settled into the back seat gingerly, trying not to imagine what other derrieres had favored these cracked vinyl seats. The cab smelled of coffee and testosterone. The officer radioed in. After he received a response, he said, "Okay, you check out clean. Step out of the car."

He flipped open a small notebook as I slipped out and began to ask me about the attack, making rapid, neat notes as I answered his questions. I went over the incident again, saddened by my pitiful lack of detail. My attacker drove away in a silver minivan. Unfortunately since all minivans looked alike to a single, childless female that was about as detailed a description as I could provide. My attacker was male and, from the trajectory of my assault, I estimated at least six-four. And strong. I looked apologetically at the officer. I made an even lousier victim than detective.

"So you believe your attack was related to your interest in your friends' recent mishaps?"

"Two people are dead. That's not a mishap, Officer. That's a tragedy."

He looked up from his notes. "Anyone you know who would like to strangle you?"

He got a grin from me on that one. "Take a number. But not anyone who would actually follow through on it."

The officer flipped closed his notebook, handed me his card. "If you thing of anything else, you can call the station. I'll make out a re-port. If there are any developments, you'll be apprised. In the meantime, you may want to leave the investigation of your two friends to the authorities."

"I did. They ruled it a murder-suicide. Wham, bam, thank you, ma'am."

"And you think differently?"

I traced my throat. "I know differently."

I went back to the limousine lot, peeled my textbook off the pavement and headed home. I took a long, hot shower to wash the night's memory off me, fell into bed and slept the sleep of someone recently assaulted, the images pop-ulating my dreams neither restful nor reassur-ing. I woke stark naked in a tangle of sheets. The clock beside my bed said 10:33. I'd had an appointment at Academic Advisory Services that morning at 10:00 a.m.

I arrived on campus at eleven-fifty. I was quickly becoming the poster child for the Ac-ademic Early Intervention System. A work-study student shredding transcripts glanced up as I came in the door.

"Hi!" I smiled breezily, coed to coed. "I re-ceived a letter asking me to stop in and have a chat with one of the advisors."

"Academic intervention candidate?"

"No, sorority sister from Hubba Hubba Thighs."

The student smiled. Anyone with a nose ring had to have a sense of humor. "Do you have an appointment?"

"Yeah, at 10:00 a.m."

The student smiled again. Coeds in arms. A woman with shoulders like a linebacker stepped out from an inner office. Her stance was stiff, as if she wore a brass-plated bustier under her Peter Pan collar. "Kaitlyn, could you please hand deliver this to the registrar's." The woman glanced at me.

"Mrs. Reynolds, this student is here for academic advisement."

The woman's gaze stopped at my bared neck. I'd figured wearing a turtleneck in July in Memphis would have caused more speculation than the bruised line circling my throat. The woman's eyes met mine with the burst blood vessel. "You have an appointment?"

"I have a 1.2 GPA."

I either scared the woman or intrigued her. I suspected the latter. A woman with brass-plated boobs doesn't scare easy. She glanced at the extralarge face of her wristwatch, then nodded.

I left twenty minutes later with an Academic Improvement Plan, the hours of the college's free tutoring assistance program and a low sense of self-esteem. Eyeballing my neck, Mrs. Reynolds also offered the contact info for the on-campus confidential counseling service. Drawing my index finger across my throat, I assured her this was a one-time deal only and the next time, I'd make sure I was packing. She ushered me out of office, fast.

On the way to my car, I heard my name and turned to find Rocco Delvecchio who had been in my Spring comp class and had an unnatural crush on me. Normally I wouldn't give a nineteen-year-old any opportunity for encouragement, but Rocco, godson of Vito Figuero's capo, had come from an even more colorful background than me. He'd already arranged a transfer plan with TennU's prelaw program when he finished his gen eds here and had a single-minded purpose rare in a person under twenty.

He took one look at my neck and emitted a low whistle through his teeth. "You in trouble, Silver?" He spoke in the low, flat accent of the street and many relatives who preferred their native language to English. His brown, thick-lashed eyes took on a soulful cast that made me wish I was eighteen.

"Did I ever introduce you to my tenant, Adrienne Bloomberg?"

"You didn't answer my question."

A lawyer already. "It's long and it's messy and even I don't understand it."

He tipped his head back to give me a hooded look. "So why would some kid?"

Rocco did have one fault. A chip on his shoulder that had gotten his nose broken more than once.

"Come over for dinner tonight. I'll introduce you to my tenant. She's brilliant and a dentist's daughter. In her second year at the university. Honors scholar. Premed." I looked over his tough exterior. "You two would be good for each other. She'll smooth some of those edges off you."

He rubbed the crooked bridge of his nose. "Yeah, what will I do for her?"

Things my thirty-something years and growing sense of morality refused to let me think about in connection with a nineteen-year-old male. "Whatever it is, I don't want details." I ripped another blank page out of my daily planner and scribbled my address and phone number on it. "You know where that is?"

He looked at the address. "I know the neighborhood. Respectable."

Not often a term I hear in reference to something connected to my person. Ah, youth. I arranged a time with Rocco and took off. I'd been running late since I woke and I still had to go to the funeral home to discuss final arrangements with Wilson Bintliff and I wanted to stop at the police station to see if any progress had been made on my case. I have the heart of an optimist.

The precinct was closer. I spoke to the front desk sergeant, was ushered in by another fresh-faced rookie. The officer who had taken my information wouldn't be back on duty until the night shift. I read a copy of his report, reviewing the incident again with its pitiful lack of clues—no identifying characteristics, no license plate, no other description except a vehicle as common as dirt. I didn't even insult the officer by asking if there were any developments.

Wilson Bintliff greeted me at the funeral home door with a professional somberness and shined Florsheims, which I found strangely comforting. He led me into his private office, discreet enough not to comment on the ring around my neck. Paul's body had been officially declared a suicide and released. As Billie had told me, there had been no evidence of anyone else in the house, and any marks on Paul's body had been consistent with death by hanging. If the police had found anything to the contrary, they were keeping it to themselves. They wanted this case to go away. I wanted to know why.

Wilson and I caught up on mutual acquaintances as I followed him down a wide stairwell to a showcase of caskets. I chose a polished rosewood model with brass trim. Stylish like my ex-husband. After Paul's death, I'd left several messages on his sister's answering machine for her to call me. It'd taken a day of telephone tag before we finally connected. After I told her the details with as much diplomacy as a family member deserved, her Southern accent had bottomed out and her voice had become hollow and hard. "Suicide is a mortal sin in the eyes of the Lord," she'd said.

At that time, Paul's death had not been officially ruled a suicide as I pointed out to her.

"My brother lived a sinner. I do not find it hard to believe he died a sinner."

"Does that mean you don't want to give the eulogy?" I'd inquired. The line had gone dead.

"We have some lovely memory cards," Wilson was saying.

Death. What a racket.

"Do you have any that resemble those little

cards they carry around on the greens to keep track of their strokes.

Poor Wilson shifted in his Florsheims, trying to decide if I was serious or not. I wasn't sure myself. Paul with his preference for red and Cajun shrimp might have enjoyed the campy detail.

Wilson tapped his long, elegant index finger against his chin. "We could set up one of those miniature putting greens. Callers could pay their respects by trying for a hole in one."

I smiled, inordinately grateful to Wilson and his shiny Florsheims. It was on my way home I wept.

Chapter Eight

"Wilson Bintliff says hello," I told Auntie Peggilee as I came into the kitchen.

"Oh, my," Auntie drawled with a long sigh that made me study her. Smiling, she applied another coat of St. Tropez Red to her fingernails.

"Did I ever tell you I slept with Wilson Bintliff?"

"You cheated on Harvey?" Harvey was Auntie's fourth and final husband.

"Goodness, no, it was after Harvey had gone to the Great Beyond. Not long, though." She blew on her nails on her right hand while she airily waved the left. "The night of the wake actually."

An image of the display room with all those satin-lined caskets popped into my mind. Auntie switched hands.

"It was only that one time. Wilson told me, though, that it happened more often than people thought."

"No wonder he's been so successful. A full-service funeral home."

Auntie held her hands at arm's length, inspected her nails. "Best thing I could have done. Got my blood pumping." She looked up from her fingertips. "You should find yourself a Wilson Bintliff. Get your mind off everything."

I opened the refrigerator, took out the pitcher of iced tea. "How do you know I didn't just get back from jumping Bintliff's bones?"

"Be better for you than running around getting your neck wrung," Auntie declared. She nodded as I held up a glass of tea. "What about that detective?"

"Ahh, Lexi," I said in my best Billie imitation.

"If I was younger, believe me, he'd keep more than just my mind occupied. He ever wear a uniform?"

"I imagine." I set her tea before her and sat down at the table.

She sipped the tea, her expression becoming glazed. "Love a man in uniform. I hyperventilate just driving by Fort Grant."

I thought of Della and her brother. Maybe I should start at the beginning with Della's brother's death, the event that triggered her descent and eventual death instead of working my way backward. The back door opened, interrupting my musings. Adrienne came in, followed by her dad.

"Ladies," Herb Bloomberg greeted us. He was round—round face, round head, round eyes, round body that made you want to stick a finger in his stomach just to see if he'd giggle. He kissed Auntie's hand first, then mine. Herb fancied himself a ladies' man. Spend too much time around tanks of nitrous oxide and you could delude yourself about anything. Not releasing my hand, his eyes zeroed in on my mouth with professional scrutiny. "Open up."

"Herb, if that's a pickup line, it's going to be a long, dry spell before you get lucky."

"Open up." He pantomimed the motion with his own mouth as he grasped my chin between his thumb and index finger and tugged down. With an annoyed look, I tipped my head and stuck out my tongue.

Herb moved in, clucked disapproval. "Your back molars are worn smooth."

He straightened. I snapped my mouth shut.

"Look at that." He tapped my jawline. "Right now your mouth's tighter than a Republican and tax cuts. Release this muscle."

I forced my mouth to relax. My teeth unclenched.

"Wear the mouth guard, Silver. Get some

chamomile tea, the loose leaves you get at the specialty shops or a health food store, not the bags. Sip a cup or two before you go to bed. It has natural relaxation properties."

"That's what I was just telling the child, Herb." Auntie entered the conversation. "She needs to relax."

"But Auntie's suggestion was a little more fun than chewing on rubber all night."

"The good Lord only gave you one set of teeth, Silver."

"It's not like I'm doing it on purpose, Herb," I defended. "I'm sleeping when I grind them. I didn't even know I was grinding them until you pointed it out." Except for the times my teeth scraped against each other so hard, it woke me up. "And that news didn't help much except to give me something else to get tense about."

"What the hell happened to your neck?" Herbie switched focus. "It looks like someone tried to strangle you."

"Someone did." I took a long, leisurely drink of tea. "Although I'm sure he wasn't the first one who'd had the impulse. He was just the first to act on it."

Herb sank down on the chair between Auntie and myself.

"What have you got yourself into now, Silver?"

I airily waved away his concern. "Some animal jumped me last night at the end of my shift at Luxury Limousine."

"Yeah, but she gouged his eyes out," Auntie said proudly.

I leaned in, earnest, "I may be a little tense for a while longer, Doc. Can I get you an iced tea?" I stood. "Adrienne?" I extended the offer to her. She was staring at my neck. She'd already been gone when I awoke.

"They're not after you now, too, are they, Silver?"

"Who's after who? What's going on?" Herb demanded, his voice taking on a parental tone.

As I sliced more lemon, Adrienne explained to her father about Della and Paul. Their deaths had each gotten a two-inch column in the daily. Herb hadn't seen the stories. When his daughter finished, Auntie supplied the details of last night's attack. I poured tea into tall glasses. At the end of the story, Herb's gaze slid to me.

"What'd you do?"

I squeezed lemon into my tea. "Asked one too many questions."

"What did your friends do?"

"That's the one too many question."

He didn't smile. Neither did I. He glanced at his daughter. "Adrienne, you need to get ready."

"You're going out tonight?" I asked her, remembering Rocco.

"A friend of the family's passed away suddenly this morning," Herb supplied. My eyebrow arched with speculation. "Heart attack." He cut me off at the pass. "The funeral is tonight."

"Did we have plans, Silver?" Adrienne asked.

"No, don't worry about it. I'd invited someone over for dinner that I wanted you to meet but we can always do it another time."

"Really?" Adrienne's long drawl revealed interest. "Friend of yours?"

"He was in my comp class. Rocco DelVecchio. Prelaw." I looked to daddy for approval.

"He doesn't sound Jewish," Herbie said dryly.

I punched his arm lightly. "Bet you'd be surprised if he was."

Herbie glanced at Adrienne and tapped his watch. "Time to go soon."

"When is he coming over?" Adrienne asked, ignoring her father.

"Around seven-thirty."

She brightened. "I could be back by then if

I skip the gathering after the burial." She looked at her father, giving him the 'little-girl' gaze that had reduced daddies' resolve for centuries. "You don't mind, do you, Daddy?"

I thought the "Daddy" was a nice touch.

"Go get ready, and we'll discuss it on the way over."

Adrienne moved toward her room, giving me the thumbs up sign above Herbie's head.

Herb waited until we heard Adrienne's bedroom door shut. He looked at me, grave-faced. "Is that the complete story?"

"For now," I replied.

"Adrienne, Peggilee—" He glanced at Auntie. "Are they in danger?"

His question gave me pause. "I don't think so." Then again I hadn't thought anyone would come after me, either, until last night. "They're not involved."

"They live with you, don't they?"

Herb had a point. Until now I hadn't considered that my nosing around could harm someone else. I suppressed the urge to touch the line on my neck, snapped the rubber band against my wrist instead.

"Don't you worry about me, Herb." Auntie stood up, her posture not unlike my advisor this morning with her full metal jacket. She went to the canvas bag on the counter that held her knitting, pulled out a length of lead pipe. "The man that put a mark on my Silver comes a-calling, he's going to be sorry."

"Not if he shoots you first," Herb pointed out with an irrefutable logic that made me twitch. His gaze moved on to me. "Or Adrienne."

For the first time, I was scared. For the people I loved. It was a feeling that went beyond twitching.

I nodded. "You're right, Herb."

"Let the police do their job, Silver." His voice held its rational level.

Serras echoed in my head.

"According to them, they already have. They're calling it a murder-suicide."

"And you think they're wrong?"

"Yes."

"Does anyone else?"

Again I thought of Serras…fondly.

"I think someone set up Paul so it would look like he murdered Della then took his own life."

Herb leaned back, folded his round fingers on his round belly, his lids half-mast in contemplation. He looked at Auntie still slapping the lead pipe against her palm from the corner of his eyes. "You agree with her, Peggi?"

Auntie gave her palm a few more solid thumps before answering. When she did speak, she looked at me, not Herb. "Silver is my heart. And I'm scared to death for her. But if I tell her to stop and she does...for me. Well, maybe she could live with it but I have a huge doubt." Auntie looked at Herb. "What I do know sure as the sun is setting right now, is that I couldn't live with it." She looked back at me, smiling. "My baby will make up her own mind."

Herb looked at me. "And what about my baby, Silver?"

He had a point. Paul and Della were dead. Nothing would change that.

"I'm ready." Adrienne came into the kitchen, freshly made-up and in respectable black that cast a pallor over her features. I renewed my resolve to wear red to Paul's service.

Herb stood, not much taller than his daughter, making it awkward when he put a pudgy arm around her shoulders. I suspected the protective gesture was as much for my benefit as it was for Adrienne. When I was twelve, my friends and I hung out at the playground–at the ball field or the swings but, most of all, in the surrounding thick stand of trees where kids could sneak smokes or gulp their parents' stolen liquor. One day I was coming out of the woods, heading home, leaving Chip Beaumont frustrated because I'd let him French kiss me but not feel me up—even at twelve, I'd had standards—when I'd seen a girl about my age coming in from the outfield, the softball game over, meeting her father who waited for her on the third baseline. Unlike Herb, the man towered over his daughter but his gesture was the same as he walked to the car with his daughter, his arm slung around her shoulders in the way of a man who loves his child. Before today, it was the last time I'd cried.

"Adrienne," I said, mentally snapping a rubber band against my brain, "Rocco can come over another time. There's no need to rush."

"It's a funeral, Silver." Adrienne pointed out. "No disrespect," she inserted for her father, "but it's not like I want to hang out." She stepped outside, her father's arm still around her and not realizing how very, very lucky she was.

As the back door slammed, I looked at Auntie across the table. "Nice speech," I told her.

"You think he bought it?"

I smiled, realizing how very, very lucky I was.

Rocco arrived at seven-twenty, smelling of soap and spice and looking like my adolescent fantasies. Auntie was similarly impressed before she left us for her monthly mahjong game. I explained to Rocco that Adrienne had an obligation but would join us shortly. I poured him a glass of tea and refilled my glass. We took our drinks out to the front porch and settled into rockers like an old married couple. We exchanged the requisite remarks about the weather. I'd seen Rocco glance at my neck several times since his arrival. I rocked slowly and waited for his questions to begin. It didn't take long.

"Are you going to tell me what happened or am I going to have to torture it out of you?" He was smiling but his eyes were serious.

Watching the setting sun, I told the story again. Rocco sipped his tea, set it on the small table between our chairs. "You work for Luxury Limousines?"

"I fill in. They call me a couple times a month, usually weekends. The tips are good, and the hours don't interfere with school."

"Did you know they're a money-laundering front?"

I looked at him blankly. "No."

"They've been part of Uncle Vito's organization for years."

Operations like Figuero's generated huge amounts of cash. Figuero can't stuff it all under his mattress but he couldn't risk becoming a prime target for the IRS, either. So he buys into a lot of legit business and distributes the illegal money among the fronts. The businesses scrupulously report every dime, but they fiddle the books to make all the profits seem to come from legitimate sources. The best businesses were cash businesses—bars, restaurants, vending machines. Limo services. I remembered Mooney standing guard last night. "What about The Oyster?"

Rocco gave me a pitying look. "Any of the major clubs in the city. No one would last as long as Uncle Vito has if he didn't have the city sewn up."

I thought of Billie, the large amounts of cash that came into the club. "Billie's?"

He shook his head. "She's one of the few independents."

I felt younger than I had in days. Still I'd seen Figuero's men in the club. I said the same to Rocco.

He shrugged. "I didn't say she didn't deal with Figuero. Just not directly."

My innocent moment ended. "How big is he?"

Rocco hesitated and I thought he wasn't going to answer. Then, he said so softly, I had to lean in to hear him. "He's big. Politicians, businessmen, prosecutors, judges, cops, court clerks." In Rocco's voice was disdain warring with the deep connection to family, the neighborhood, blood.

"How does he get these people in his pocket?" Sure, I knew the stories, but I'd never heard them from someone so close to the source.

Rocco's dark, hooded eyes stayed steady on mine. "He learns your desire. Ambition, power, money, sex. Then he gives it to you." His tone held the weary reality of an older man. "Until he owns you."

"Then what?" I wanted him to go on.

"Then you do what he says."

"No one's ever been able to touch him?"

"The local cops don't have the manpower or the resources."

"What about the Feds?"

Rocco shrugged again. "Maybe, but Uncle Vito is too smart and well-insulated."

"Are you saying he's untouchable?"

Rocco looked at the setting sun. "No one's untouchable."

We sat on the porch, rocking gently while the sun turned a heartbreaking orange-pink, and we thought of evil.

"So the police know about Figuero's money-laundering fronts?" I was thinking of Serras's surprise visit last night. I'd thought Billie had sent him. What if it had been someone else?

Rocco reached for his tea. "Of course. They just can't prove it."

I thought of Billie's story about Serras. If it had happened as she said, he was a hero. But it could as easily have been a set-up. It was Serras's word and a million dollars that said the veteran cop had pulled out the dealer's gun to make it look like a shootout between the dealer and Serras—kill them both and take off with the million dollars. Yeah, it could have been a set-up but my instincts told me I was wrong. That the story had gone down as described and Serras was a clean cop. Then again, these were the same instincts that had let me believe marriage would make Paul faithful and Luxury Limos specialized in limousines, not money laundering.

On the other hand, from Serras's perspective, I don't exactly fare lily-white. Coed or not, I'd gone from a strip club to a Figuero operation, becoming a prime connection between two murders along the way. Wasn't exactly a Doris Day musical.

The sun was at the skyline when Adrienne's

Jetta came down the street and rolled into the driveway, giving a perky double honk as it passed us on the porch. The high color in Adrienne's cheeks as she came around the front and up the porch steps said she'd worked herself up into a blind date dither. Rocco rose as she stepped onto the porch. I made the introductions, offered Adrienne my rocker, angling it closer toward Rocco. Rocco took in Adrienne with a gentleman's gaze, lightly holding the hand she'd offered. I left them on the pretense of getting more tea for everyone.

On my way to the kitchen, I hummed, my belief in my instinctive powers restored. I was still humming, bent over at the refrigerator, selecting a lemon from the bottom crisper drawer when I heard the front door slam and footsteps headed my way.

"No need to help," I admonished as I straightened. "I've got everything under—"

Before I could say control, a strong hand clasped my shoulder and spun me face-to-face with my favorite local law enforcer. Serras's dark gaze came down hard on the bruised line of flesh across my throat. His other hand clasped my shoulder, and he shook me a little as he muttered a Greek epitaph.

"Are you trying to get yourself killed?"

Before I could answer, that mouth that had probably dominated more women's fantasies than I cared to consider came down on mine. The kiss was as hard as the man, without a touch of tenderness that would have had me pushing him away and sorely disappointed. I came to him openmouthed, his tongue thrusting into me deep only to be drawn in further. We were way past preliminaries. We indulged ourselves thirty seconds, maybe a minute, his hands fisting into the length of my hair and my body meeting his, sensation for sensation. When it was over, I released him as suddenly as he'd taken me. I took a ragged, dissatisfied breath, knowing I would yearn for more for a long time.

He looked down at me. "Another dancer from the Oyster. They found her dead this afternoon. Strangled. Lucy Champlain."

I wanted to stumble back, seek support from the tall appliance behind me. I locked my knees, ignoring their shameful weakness and stood without assistance.

"I just saw her. Last night." I kept my voice factual.

Serras rubbed his gorgeous Greek brow. "I know. One of the other dancers said she saw Lucy talking to a redhead in hot pants with a white stretch limo."

Okay, inconspicuous I'm not. I saw Lucy's thin face, the meager gold chain around her ankle that had glinted as she'd tapped her heel against the street.

"She has kids," I remembered.

"They came home from school. And found her."

"Oh." The squeak that escaped my mouth sounded like a small animal caught in a trap. I saw Serras's hands spread, lift an inch, readying to catch me. Sadness now mingled with shame that I had ever doubted him.

"Someone must think she knew something." His index finger drew a soft line beneath my throat's bruised flesh. "They now think you knew it, too."

"I asked her if she remembered anything about the call she overheard Della making the night she got killed. At first, she gave me the murder-suicide song and dance but when I dropped her off, I don't know, maybe she was grateful for the ride." My voice cracked. I took a breath, gathering my resources. "Before she went inside her house, she told me that after Della made the call she must have thrown away the phone because Lucy had seen it in the garbage."

"So there'd be no evidence of the call. Did she say anything else? A number? A name?"

I shook my head. "It's all she gave me. It's not much. Not worth getting killed over." I glanced away from Serras. "Where are her kids?"

"At her sister's."

I still couldn't look at him. "Most of the girls called in sick at the Oyster the day after Della's death. Lucy worked a double. Last night it was late. I just wanted to give her a ride home."

"Silver."

Something in the way he said my name allowed me to look at him.

"You didn't kill her."

"Who did?"

"Silver?" Adrienne's soft voice came from the doorway. "Is everything okay?"

I looked at her, then back at Serras. Slowly I shook my head.

Chapter Nine

I convinced Serras to stay for supper, then shooed him and Adrienne back to the porch with a fresh pitcher of iced tea. Supper was going to be a simple affair. T-bones, Caesar salad, twice-baked potatoes. I had planned on peach melba shortcakes for dessert but the events of the past few minutes demanded the intricacies of chocolate mousse. I was separating the egg whites when Adrienne came in, put a hand on my shoulder. I jumped. The egg slipped from my hand to the floor.

"Shoot," Adrienne declared. "I didn't mean to scare you."

I stared down as the egg spread across the floor like an inland amoeba and, for the first time, feared I wasn't going to remain intact. Funny the things that can set you off. I went for my wrist for a good ol' stinging supersnap but I saw Adrienne watching me, her expression far too worried for someone so young with a nine-teen-year-old hotcake rocking twenty feet away.

"Not a problem." I shifted into efficiency mode, grabbing the salt shaker. I squatted down and sprinkled salt like a domestic dervish atop the yellow and clear goo. "Saw this on a cooking show. Always wanted to try it. Supposed to soak up the slime. Make cleanup a breeze." I was talking too fast, too high, like a housewife on helium.

Adrienne knelt down beside me with a fist-ful of paper towels and watched me eye level. I suspected Serras had told her about Lucy. The kindness in her gaze told me she understood. Competence was the only thing keeping me in control at the moment.

"What do you think of Rocco?" I said girl to girl, heading off any discussion of less pleasant subjects.

Adrienne smiled with a hint of ultrafeminine shyness that told me my work there was done. I smiled back, optimism seeping back into my weary being.

The salt trick worked as promised. My optimism level spiked. I discarded the paper towels and turned to the block of bittersweet chocolate on the cutting board. "You get your perky butt back out there, then. Pronto. There's salsa in the fridge. Chips in the cupboard above the dishwasher. You return bearing food, and they'll both fall in love with you."

"They can miss me for a few minutes," she said with the attitude that comes from living with an ex-stripper and her auntie whose idea of growing old gracefully is wearing matching push-up bras and thong undies.

"They're having a grand time comparing street stories. All I've got is a few tales of bas mitzvahs gone bad. Besides I slipped away—"

Her hand rested on my shoulder once more. She wasn't done with me yet. I put the chopped chocolate, water, and a shot of brandy into the top of a double boiler.

"To share something interesting with you."

I stirred, waited.

"At the service, I ran into an old Saturday school chum. Marcie Armstrong. It's been two nose jobs since I've seen her."

I smiled, proud of my girl.

"Marcie was full of fun facts. During the reciting of the Kaddish, I couldn't get her to shut up."

Still smiling a small smile, I added unsalted butter to the melted chocolate.

"Seems the grieving widow has a passion for golf. She took private lessons several times a week."

I gave Adrienne an oblique glance. She arched one brow, giving her a sly, self-satisfied expression. "At the Meadows." She paused for drama. "With your ex-husband."

The water in the bottom of the double boiler began to bubble too hard. I grabbed the pot off the burner and stirred hard to prevent the chocolate from burning.

I glanced at Adrienne. "Coincidence?" I ventured.

She snorted in perfect imitation of Auntie.

I set the chocolate aside to cool and moved on to the egg whites. "Paul slept with a lot of women, Adrienne. And well-to-do Memphis matrons were his specialty." I shrugged.

"Okay." Adrienne began ladling salsa into a bowl. I finished whipping the egg whites, moved onto the whipping cream. "How 'bout this? According to Marcie Armstrong, the official word is that Bennie Herschmann died of a heart attack, but the rumor is that he killed himself."

I stopped whipping.

"By hanging."

God bless Marcie Armstrong. "Is that the reason for the quickie burial?"

She dipped a chip into salsa and munched. "The burial? No, that's not unusual. Jewish tradition is for burial to take place as soon as possible, on the same day of the death if possible, no more than two nights after, at the most. It's considered disrespectful to the deceased to delay the burial."

"Did you see the body?"

"There is no wake. No open casket. The body is not put on display. Jewish law."

"In the case of sudden death, especially suspicious, wouldn't an autopsy be performed?"

"Against Jewish law." She bit into another chip.

"Was the body cremated?"

"Again, not allowed in the Jewish religion."

"So there's no proof except Marcie Armstrong's rumor radar."

"Not to be discounted. If it wasn't for her, our Saturday temple class would still believe Kimberly Feldman's 36 Ds were the result of a summer growth spurt."

"With all due respect to Marcie's marvelous mouth, we need more."

"So, we'll get it," Adrienne said with the cockiness of youth.

"No." I concentrated on slowly pouring the melted chocolate into the bowl with the egg yolks mixed with sugar. When I finished, I found Adrienne looking at me, the disappointment in her eyes overtaking the sparkle put there by Rocco.

"No?"

"There was another death last night. It was almost two." I folded in egg whites, letting the fact sink in.

"Your father is right." Tactical error, I realized as a long-suffering expression glazed Adrienne's face. Never propose a parent is right to an individual under twenty-one.

Whipped cream was needed. I folded it in with the slow, skilled movements of a Frenchman making love. "People are getting killed, Adrienne. If anything happened to you or Auntie…"

Adrienne released a short hoot of disbelief.

My gaze hit her dead-on. "The closest I want you to danger is rocking right now on our front porch." I handed her the chips and salsa. She took them but didn't move, as if debating whether to argue more. Instead she leaned in and pecked a quick kiss on my cheek, then moved off, humming "The Battle Hymn of the Republic." *Youth.*

I was spooning the mousse into cobalt-blue dessert dishes when Serras came in, leaned against my counter. I flashed him a hostess's smile, scraping the last of the mousse into a dish and setting the bowl into the sink. The smile he gave me back had nothing to do with propriety.

I picked up two dessert dishes, opened the refrigerator door, set the dishes inside to chill. "How are things going out there?" I cocked my head toward the front porch.

"You get a kick out of getting involved in other people's lives, don't you?"

"You know me, Serras." I turned back to find him too close, handing me two more of the mousses. I wrapped my hands around them, meeting his fingertips. "Control. That's what it's all about." I pulled away from his touch, set the dishes on the refrigerator shelf.

"Is that why you're studying accounting? Profits. Losses. Expenses. Assets. Neat columns where everything adds up."

I said nothing. I was waiting to see where he was going with this. Certainly there are sexier ways of seducing a woman than psychoanalyzing her. I suspected Serras knew this.

"Then, there's the dancing onstage. You determine when, how much is revealed. How close someone will come. Your audience goes away, satisfied they've seen you at your most vulnerable. In reality, they've seen you at your most guarded. Your most powerful.

"But the deaths of Della, Paul, Lucy. They

don't add up into a tidy column, do they? That's why you're so determined to find out who killed them and why."

I shut the refrigerator door carefully, resisting the urge to slam it. *Control.* Irritation grew inside me. No one likes to be so obvious. "Ahh, the psyche of the stripper. You were doing good up until the end, Detective. Still I'll bet you could take it on the road, at least get a spot on a call-in radio show."

"Yeah?" He went for the mousse that had escaped the rubber spatula, scraped a fingerful from the sides of the bowl. "Where did I go wrong?"

"I'm done detecting." I busied myself gathering utensils, bowls, beaters off the counter. "I don't want anyone else hurt. No, let me rephrase that. I don't want anyone else killed." With a grand sweep of my arm, I sent everything clattering into the sink. Serras grabbed my wrist right above the rubber band. I stared down at his fingers aligned above the elastic.

"Problem is you may not have that choice any longer."

I raised my gaze.

"Whoever is behind this thinks Lucy shared something with you."

"Yeah, well, they won't have to do Chinese

water torture on me to learn what I know. Della called someone, then threw away the phone. For all we know, her cell phone contract had expired."

"But Lucy must have known more. A great deal more, and whoever visited her today, suspects you know it, too."

His grip on my wrist relaxed, his touch gentled. Hell, Serras, I thought, it's been a long day. Don't get tender on me now.

"That's all Lucy told you?"

And I was worried Serras was going sappy on me. Make a man chocolate mousse and you suffer the consequences. I pulled my arm away from him, offered him the mousse mixing bowl and a spatula as a reward.

"You think I'm withholding information?" I made my voice indignant but I had to smile as he cleaned the bowl. I filled the sink with soapy water, began washing the bowls and utensils. "I wish she had said more."

Serras added the scraped bowl to the sink of soapy water. "How many times have you gone to your ex-husband's house?"

He'd caught me off guard. It was intentional. "Technically it's now my house."

"But you didn't know that the first time you crossed the death scene."

Busted. I'd first gone back to the house the day I found Paul. I had Paul's keys in my purse and a puzzle I needed to solve. I only wanted to take a look around, I told myself. A prosecutor would call it trespassing. It wasn't the first time in my life I'd walked a fine line.

It had been past dusk. I had cruised the upscale neighborhood but didn't see any black-and-whites, anonymous vans, unmarked sedans. I parked by a cluster of building lots ready for the next phase of development and walked to Paul's house, slipping around the side to the back door. The door didn't have a police seal but the knob had a gritty residue where the crime techs had dusted for prints.

I'd stood for a long time in the center of the great room with the vaulted ceiling, wondering why. Then I'd searched the rooms, the drawers, the closets, the cupboards, looking for an answer.

I'd found nothing.

That's what I told Serras now.

"You were one of the last people to see two of the three murdered people alive. The other one lists you as an emergency contact. You were in the second victim's house the day of his death. Somebody's looking for something and they think you either have it or know where it is."

"But I don't."

He grabbed the dish towel draped in the refrigerator door handle and began to dry the dishes in the drainer with quick swipes.

"You don't have to do—" I turned to him and saw the smear of chocolate mousse at the corner of his mouth, totally defeating his irate expression "–those."

"I know." He continued to dry.

"The next cupboard over," I said as he searched for the right shelf to put a bowl away.

"My mother used to make me do this every night. She'd wash. I'd dry. God, I hated that." The lines in his face eased slightly. "As I got older, I suspected she used to purposefully dirty more dishes than necessary just to keep me in the kitchen longer. Have a chance to talk to me."

"I'll bet you were a rotten kid."

"The worst," he confirmed. His shoulders relaxed. The quick smile he gave me said he didn't regret one minute of it.

"Then Royce Ealy straightened you out."

He lowered his lids to half-mast. "You been checking me out, LeGrande?"

I stacked a bowl on top of another one in the drainer. "Know thy enemy."

His face sobered. "I'm not the enemy, Silver." He traced my bruised flesh. "This is the enemy."

"Just being careful, Serras."

He took my wet wrist. "I know. Comes with the territory." He lightly snapped my rubber band, released my hand. He picked up a wire whip, shook the drops of water off it into the sink, then brushed a towel over it. "Royce and my father had been partners. As I got older, I realized Royce had a thing for my mother, too, but he never acted on it. Out of respect for my father."

"Your father was killed by an intruder in your house?"

Serras's expression shut down. He said nothing, only nodded.

"Did your mother ever remarry?"

Again he only shook his head.

"Is she still alive?" I persisted, curious about his unexpected reticence.

"Passed away two years ago. Breast cancer." He held up the double boiler.

"Bottom cupboard next to the stove." I had finished the dishes and was rinsing the romaine for the salad. "No brothers, sisters?" I tore the Romaine leaves into a wooden bowl.

Serras shook his head. "Mom miscarried twice before she had me. Her pregnancy with me was difficult. The doctor advised no more pregnancies. Still she tried. She got pregnant again two years later but the pregnancy didn't go full term. The baby was born eight weeks premature. A girl. They tried to save her. She hung on for almost a week. Afterward, Mom got her tubes tied." He shut the cupboard door. "How 'bout you?"

I had no choice. I'd started it. "My mother never married." I got out Worcestershire, lemon juice, an egg, Dijon mustard. "Carnival came to town for four days. When it pulled out, she was pregnant with me. The man she'd slept with worked the midway. He had a French accent," I added as if that explained everything. "And my mother would say she never regretted it one second in her entire life."

"One great love?" Serras speculated.

I smiled, forgetting Serras had never met my mother. "More of a case of one great spin on the Tilt-A-Whirl." I leaned down to get a small pan, enjoying too much Serras's laughter. That's the problem with talking. No matter how careful you are, some of the deep truth about yourself slips out and then bam, there's a connection.

"Adrienne mentioned something interesting to me when she got back tonight from the funeral of a family friend." Time to get back to business. "Seems the widow was an avid golfer, a member of the Meadows where she frequently took private lessons." I put a small pan of water on the stove to coddle the egg.

Serras's drying motions slowed. "She was sleeping with your ex-husband?"

"Rumor has it, along with the fact her husband didn't die of a heart attack as reported. He hung himself."

Serras processed the information. "Who's the deceased?"

I thought a minute. "Hermann, Herbert. Herschmann. Ben Herschmann."

Serras took a small notebook from his back pocket, flipped it open, wrote down the name. "She know him well?"

"You can ask her but I don't think so. I got the impression he was more a friend of her father's, and Adrienne went along to pay her respects and support her dad."

"She say how the widow was reacting?"

"She didn't say." The water on the stove began to boil. I added the egg, set the microwave time for forty-five seconds. "You'll have to ask her."

He closed the notebook, slid it back into his pocket. The dishes were done. He folded the towel neatly, hung it back on the refrigerator door.

"Anything else I can do?"

I looked at him, his to-die-for features made accessible by a smear of chocolate mousse and my realization of the man's loneliness. He'd never admit it and I'd never call him on it, but I knew. The simple pleasure of coming home, drying dishes, talking to a woman had not been his for a long time.

"You know anything about grills?"

"I'm a man, aren't I? We're born with a grilling gene."

"Good. Go light the one in the backyard." The microwave timer went off. I took the pan off the burner, scooped out the egg.

"Serras?"

He stopped, turned at the door. I walked over. "You've got a little something." I stood on tiptoe, brought my lips to the corner of his mouth, licked away the spot of mousse. "Right there."

He smiled down at me. "Knock it off, LeGrande."

My pleased laugh followed him as he walked out the door.

Later that evening, the four of us sat around the dining table, the remains of the meal spread before us. I had planned on coffee and dessert on the porch, but our bellies full, we had leaned back against our chairs and lingered. And I was loath to hasten the process that would result in the inevitable, "It's getting late," or "Tomorrow's another day," or any of those inanities to remind us this was only a temporary reprieve.

Serras looked across the table at Adrienne. "Silver tells me a friend of your family's passed away. My condolences."

Until that time we had not talked of death or murder or funerals as if a silent pact had been made among all parties for a few hours to only be four people come together to share a meal and each other's company.

The spell cast somewhere between Caesar salad and rare, grilled sirloin cracked. Still I rose to make fresh-ground French roast, determined the evening could still be salvaged by caffeine and chocolate.

Adrienne acknowledged Serras's sympathy with a slow nod. "Did she tell you his wife liked to hang out on the greens with a certain country club pro?"

Even Rocco leaned in. Sex and death, I thought. Never let it be said I didn't know how to throw a dinner party.

"She mentioned it." Serras had segued into his cool cop mode but he wasn't fooling me for a moment. He had a fire in that flat belly of his. "She said the deceased's name was Ben Herschmann.

Adrienne nodded.

"What did he do?" Serras had the grace not to flip out his fat, little notebook, although I could almost feel his fingers itching for it.

"I don't know really. He had his own company. Whatever he did, I know he did very well at it."

Serras filed the information away. I spooned real whipped cream on the chocolate mousse.

"There was some speculation about the cause of his death?" Serras asked.

"The party line was a sudden heart attack." Adrienne snapped her fingers. "But the word round the kugel was suicide. Rumor has it Ben Herschmann hung himself."

"Maybe he was depressed," Serras suggested. "The family covers it up to avoid embarrassment."

Adrienne narrowed her gaze on Serras. "And his wife just happens to have been having an affair with a man found swinging from his rafters last week."

My hostess instinct told me it was time for the chocolate mousse. I moved in with the cobalt-blue dessert dishes. "Coffee's almost done," I announced. My company looked up at me as if I were crazy.

"What was the wife's behavior like at the service?" Serras turned his attention back to Adrienne.

"Silent, straight-backed, dry-eyed. Some would say she was putting up a brave front. But those who know her know it's no front. The woman has ice water in her veins."

"Some people don't like to put on a display."

"Some people don't have their husband and lover taken out a few days apart from each other."

"Speculation. That's all you've got," Serras countered.

Adrienne raised a large spoonful of mousse. "But you'll check it out," she challenged.

Their gazes held as Adrienne drew the spoonful of mousse into her mouth. She had lived with me for over a year and was a quick study. Rocco was completely impressed. She pulled the spoon out of her mouth. "Unofficially, of course."

Serras savored his own chocolate mousse with painfully slow appreciation before he smiled at Adrienne and said, "I'll put it in my big book of clues."

More and more I feared I'd met my match.

Rocco and Adrienne left not long after coffee and dessert for a late show and what I suspected would be a heavy petting session. Serras insisted on staying to help me clean up. I wrote it off as waxing reminiscent about his memories with his mother and tried not to entertain the idea he also didn't want the evening to end.

Still as I walked with him to his car, I sensed the solitude in the man and suspected his nights, like mine, were longer than his days. He turned to me and said, "Thank you," with a thick sincerity so unlike the Serras I knew. I was about to cave, ask him to stay with me for many reasons, least of which was we both deserved not to be alone. But even as the invitation formed in my thoughts, I knew it wasn't enough. Not for Serras. Not for me. Nothing like a burgeoning sense of moral consciousness to pull the plug on a party.

Until he leaned in and kissed me long and hard, wiping out all thoughts of integrity. I was about to drag him inside, cavewoman style when headlights swept over us. Auntie's third husband's yellow Lincoln Continental pulled into the drive like a small barge, its wide body and rear fins mocking our modern, fuel-efficient, aerodynamic models. Serras and I pulled apart like teenagers caught making out in the family den.

Serras looked down at me. He didn't do any of those things that make a good girl tingle and a bad girl pant. He didn't brush my cheek, stroke away stray strands of hair from my face, whisper I was beautiful while tracing the line of my collarbone with a light fingertip. He only looked down at me for a long moment, then said, "Good night."

I blessed him, even knowing I would not sleep tonight. But I strongly suspected neither would he.

Serras shot Auntie a wave as he opened his car door. I walked back to the house as he pulled away.

Auntie met me at the front steps. "Sorry about the Continental interruptus, but I'm glad to see my earlier lecture hadn't fallen on deaf ears. About time you started listening to me."

I opened the front-screened door for us. "It was the job that brought him here, the sirloin and mousse that made him stay. There's been another murder," I told her as we moved into the kitchen. "A girl that worked at the Oyster with Della. She was strangled today in her own house. Her kids came home from school and found her."

I sat down at the kitchen table, not even the lingering sensations of Serras's skilled lips saving me now. Auntie stood, listening.

"I'd just seen her last night. She was ending her shift at the Oyster. I was waiting for my fares. I gave her a ride home in the limo. I took the long way around to her building."

Auntie walked over and stroked my hair. "So she knew kindness before she died." I moved into a tailspin.

"Serras thinks she must have known something more than that. Someone must have seen her climb into the limo and was afraid she'd told me something."

"What?" Auntie asked.

"I don't know, but they're looking for something and they think I might have it. Then Adrienne came home tonight from the funeral with some interesting information." I told Auntie about the speculation surrounding Herschmann's sudden death and his wife's fondness for a certain good-looking country club pro.

"Goodness." Auntie poured herself a cup of lukewarm coffee and plopped down in the kitchen chair across from me. "Even the good Lord rested after the sixth day. Doesn't the Devil ever take a day off?"

"If he does, it wasn't today."

Nor, I suspected, would it be tomorrow.

Chapter Ten

Serras showed the next day at Paul's funeral. So did Ben Herschmann's widow along with a whole contingent of coiffured, well-taken-care-of women from the club. Men were there too—husbands, clients, bourbon buddies from the nineteenth hole, but it was the women, their features tight and their faces tipped upward so their tears would angle back and not ruin their make up, that were most impressive that morning. I was not the only one in red. Billie had refused but Auntie, Adrienne and I had complied. But there were others, too. Paul, aware his hedonistic lifestyle would lead to an early demise, must have made his wishes known often enough that even when spoken in jest, the idea had eventually been taken seriously. The more insecure women wore burgundy or crimson but the bolder wore the red that would have made Paul smile with the pure pleasure that was both his asset and his undoing. I longed for a camera to send a picture of Paul's flock to his sister to show her there are all types of worship.

Ben Herschmann's widow wore scarlet. She was a striking blonde with the remote, arrogant facial expression of owning great wealth and the boredom that comes with it. From a distance she could pass for thirty, but close up I saw around her eyes the crepey flesh of the early forties that would send her to the plastic surgeon in the next few years. Her hand was cold when she shook mine to offer her sympathies, and her eyes had the flat translucence of a dead cod. She may have been on medication to cope with her recent circumstance. Still I had no doubt this lady could lose both her husband and her lover in the span of a few days and still make her Pilates class the next afternoon. I couldn't help but like her.

"Without your husband, the world will be a more sober place, Mrs. LeGrande."

I burst out laughing, drawing more curious, concerned glances than when I'd arrived in low-cut red silk. Ben Herschmann's widow smiled, confirming her comment's double entendre and her appreciation that I'd enjoyed it.

"My condolences on your loss also, Mrs. Herschmann."

Only a flicker of surprise broke past the

blonde's inbred composure. "Did you know Ben?"

"Not personally. Herb Bloomberg's daughter, Adrienne, rents from me. She told me last night about your husband's unexpected passing. That you were able to muster the strength to come here today, given your own personal circumstance, would have meant much to Paul."

"I understand the importance of paying respects, Mrs. LeGrande."

"Please call me Silver. Did you know Paul long?"

"My husband and I were already members of the club when he came aboard." She elegantly brushed back a side bang that fell across her forehead with perfect carelessness. "When was that? Six? Seven years ago?"

"But it was only in the last year you slept with him?" I ventured.

She smiled. I could tell she liked me also. "Last six months. He approached me. Not that the thought hadn't crossed my mind, but things like that, the complications, the logistics…" She made an airy pass with her hand. "Generally they aren't worth the trouble."

"But not this time?"

Some of the remoteness left her eyes. "You were married to him. You tell me."

I glanced at Paul flat on his back for viewing. The alcohol would have eventually done its damage but for now, even with the pancake makeup and expression of false serenity, he looked much too young and handsome to be spread out in a polished hardwood box.

I smiled at Ben Herschmann's widow. "It was worth the trouble."

"I was not foolish enough to be flattered by his initial attentions. I am attractive for my age but that age is not twenty. I assumed my husband had persuaded Paul to keep an eye on me."

She looked like the type of woman who needed an eye kept on her. I did not necessarily think it an insult.

"Had he?"

"Yes. My husband feared I was having him followed by a private detective."

"Were you?"

"No," she answered ruefully as if disappointed in herself. "Again, not that I hadn't considered it. It probably would have come to that at some time or another. There's only so much plastic surgery and a daily B-12 cocktail can do. But I figured I had a few years before I had to start compiling a portfolio to protect my assets."

"So you started sleeping with Paul for the fun of it?"

Ben Herschmann's widow smiled prettily, and in that moment she could have passed for twenty. "It was fun," she confirmed. "The most goddamn fun I ever had." With her youthful smile, she looked over her shoulder at Paul laid out like the Thanksgiving turkey. I knew she would not cry. Neither would I. I also realized, in her way, this woman had loved Paul. As had I.

"And I want you to laugh when I tell you this because I laugh myself, laugh my goddamn head off every time I think of it. I fell in love with the flipping bastard. How's that for poetic justice?"

My insight had been right. Her voice had retained the even, almost lyrical modulation that made her profanity sound like poetry and totally acceptable. Again, I suspected she might have dropped a Xanax or two to smooth out the rough edges. Behind her, people were eyeing us, the line of guests waiting to express their own sentiments lengthening. Still I doubted any sentiments to come would be as interesting as Ben Herschmann's widow.

"Mrs. Herschmann—"

"Fiona," she insisted with another elegant wave of her hand.

"Your husband's passing?" From the corner of my eye, I'd been aware of Serras watching us the whole time. A rare pang of guilt shot through me, but it was quickly displaced by my need to find out who killed Della, Paul and now Lucy. Obviously, I wasn't done detecting. "It was sudden, also, wasn't it?"

She shrugged. "Cholesterol hovering at three hundred. Two packs of cigarettes and a pitcher or two of Manhattans a day. Sure it was sudden, but the signs were all there. Ben was a heart attack waiting to happen."

Either Marcie's marvelous mouth had been mistaken or Fiona was lying. If so, why? She certainly did not seem like the type to hide anything.

"You spent a lot of time with Paul. Were you surprised when you heard about his suicide?"

Her hand was still cold and her eyes glassy as she folded her fingers around mine once more. "I'm rarely surprised, Silver."

"Paul seemed suicidal?" I tightened my own fingers on hers, not letting her go.

"No, but the man drank two liters of vodka on a good day. That doesn't necessarily imply the picture of tranquility." Still holding my hand, she turned her full gaze to Paul. When she looked at me again, regret had altered the unbroken relief of her patrician features. "I'm really going to miss that bastard."

Paul would have been proud.

Fiona glided away, the loose-limbed ease of her walk convincing me she'd been spoon-fed sedatives. Still I believed her sentiments were sincere. Serras stepped into my direct line of sight. He had watched the entire exchange. He did not look happy.

I wore the requested red to Paul's funeral, ate Cajun shrimp afterward at the club but I did not dance. Nor did I cry. It was a small, select group that gathered at Billie's. The women had paid their homage. Others from the country club set had come to the funeral as a matter of protocol. Paul's drinking buddies had come to pay their respects but also anticipated the prospect of a party after. They were now eulogizing Paul with shots of Johnny Black and pitchers of Molson Gold. Two funerals close together, not to mention Lucy's upcoming service, had wearied Billie along with the rest of us. We sat among the green and gold and deep purple of the club's interior, the Mardi Gras dolls mocking our mood with their fixed mischievous smiles.

"I saw you talking to Fiona Herschmann." Adrienne popped a shrimp into her mouth. "What did you think of her?"

"She's not what I expected." Then again, little had been this past week.

"You could reach out and grab hold of the reaction when she walked into that room. Betcha most of the women didn't even make it back to their cars before they had their cell phones out and their comments catting up the wires. I say she showed up just to spite them." Adrienne smiled. I could see she was as smitten as I was by Fiona Herschmann.

"She told me she fell in love with Paul."

"Her and half the country club." Adrienne popped another shrimp. Her eyes twinkled. "Man must have been a tiger."

Out of deference to Serras, I deliberately ignored the opening. A man who had dried my dishes deserved that much. I'd looked at him too much today—the long, dark, curling hair only a plainclothes could get away, the strong mouth, heavy lids. From the beginning I hadn't denied I'd sleep with him. The question was when.

"What did you think of the merry widow Herschmann?" I asked him. I'd known he'd come to the funeral on business. In a case of foul play, those who showed up at the service were as significant as those who didn't. He had talked at length with Fiona.

He sipped his Scotch. "I think she's a tiger."

I smiled, agreeing. "She says her husband had a heart attack."

"With all due respect to Marcie," he tipped his glass to Adrienne, "so does the death certificate."

"Fiona has a lot of money. Death certificates can be altered."

"Why?"

"To avoid scandal."

"The widow Herschmann does not seem the type to shy away from scandal."

I had to agree with him again. "Life insurance policies don't pay on a suicide."

"That's true. But unless they suspect foul play, and without anything more than a mean rumor, Ben Herschmann will take the truth with him to the grave."

Maybe Ben Herschmann had died of a heart attack, and Paul had chosen a more direct route to death than drinking. Maybe Della and Lucy had shared a penchant for kinky sex and taken it too far. Or chosen the wrong man. A man who liked it rough. A man they couldn't say no to without consequences. Maybe I could convince myself of all of the above if it wasn't for the bruise around my neck.

I stared at Serras across the table. *Careful,*

chère. He's a dangerous man. He watched me as if he read my thoughts. Busted for excessive force. Shot his partner point blank in the face. I had tasted the exquisite violence of his kiss, the rough, fierce feel of his touch. And had yearned for more. Even now, as the cold finger of suspicion trailed down my spine, I wanted him. As much as I wanted the truth.

Someone had selected a slow love song on the jukebox. I stood up, stretched out my hand to Serras. I would dance after all. For Paul. For Della. For Lucy. For myself.

On the dance floor, Serras slipped his arms around me, pressed me tight to him without apology. I gripped his back, the line of his shoulder holster beneath my fingers, the hard bulge of his gun against my breast.

"You're frightened, LeGrande," he said in a rough whisper, his breath hot against my cheek. "You're too close." We had begun to move as one in a lazy shuffle. "The control is slipping. It's about to snap."

My hand, hidden by our bodies melded tight, slid over the warning hardness of his gun, the flat plane of his abdomen until I found him full and straining. "I say when, Serras." My palm cupped him, my fingers kneaded skillfully, the vicious tension of his body threatening to take me down with him. "Remember?"

"Go ahead, LeGrande," he murmured, his voice amazingly calm considering five-foot-eleven of female could only get any closer by crawling inside him. "Talk tough. Stay in character for the next century. It doesn't matter. I still see it."

I had stilled my manipulations. He had me listening. "What do you see, Serras?"

"The loneliness. The need. The feeling of being separate."

Now he truly had me frightened. "You see all that, Serras? How?"

"Because I know it, too."

I dropped my head to his chest. I had worn red, eaten Cajun shrimp, danced. I would not cry. I fisted my hands into his shirtfront.

"Take me home, Serras."

Only the exposing streetlights and the delicious twist of tension took us that far without shedding our clothes in the street. He pulled up into a neighborhood not far from the river but far enough for a detective's salary. He jerked open the car door, pulled me up to him. My body slammed against him, my mouth already opened for his hot, brutal assault. He kicked the car door closed. Our mouths still joined, he half carried, half dragged me to the building and up the stairs to his apartment.

His body pressing mine against the hard length of the front door, he unlocked it, twisted the knob and we stumbled, almost falling inside. He yanked me up, shoving me against the back of the door, tearing at red silk that fell easily from my body beneath his fierce touch. I tugged his shirt from his waistline, my fingers clumsy, impatient, as I unlatched his belt, unsnapped his pants. His mouth moved down, grazing my skin, the slope of my breasts, kissing them, closing over a hardened nipple until I was beneath his lips, inside his mouth, against his tongue. I grasped the doorknob, braced my back against the wall to keep from buckling.

His mouth moved on, suckling, his teeth nipping. I pushed down his shirt, anxious to touch only hot flesh and hard muscle. My hand slid down, stopped on the cold metal of his gun. He hit a release, the holster unfastened, the gun slipped off and, with the care of a professional, he placed the holster on the table near the door with one hand while his other hand fondled my breast, played across my rib cage.

He turned me until I faced the door. His hands braceleted my wrists, brought my arms up above my head. My forearms pressed against the door.

My fingers gripped the jamb as his hands reached around me, cupped my breasts, then sliding down over my belly, slipped between my thighs, finding me moist and heavy. I wore no panties. Only a black garter belt and sheer stockings.

His hips thrust against me, his erection nestled against my bottom while his fingers fondled me until my own hips began to move, pushing against his hand, and my hands closed into small, drumming fists against the door as a hard, thick throbbing built. I came, my back arching and my body jerking spasmodically against Serras's hard chest, the rush of pleasure suddenly splintered by a flash of memory.

A cord around my neck, a stranger yanking me, the noose tightening. Was this what it was like? The slow-motion spasms, the writhing, twisting, the fingers curling, the fingernails cutting into the palms. Thoughts explode in the brain. The body moves with a mind of its own. Control, consciousness fading beneath a shuddering sweep of darkness. Was this what Della, Paul, Lucy had known?

I collapsed against the hard door, panting, shivering, spent. Serras's hands were light on my shoulders as he turned me to him, gathered me in his arms and held me tight against his chest. He stroked my hair gently. He'd been right. I was frightened as hell.

What he didn't know was that that had never stopped me in the past.

My hands slipped around his back, enjoying the thick muscles against my palms. My fingers played down either side of his spine, caressed his buttocks, then encircled him, stroked him. I could feel the tension, vicious inside him, building as my head dropped to nibble on his chest. The tip of my tongue ran a line down, up his abdomen. He groaned, yanking my head back by the hair and plundering my mouth as we both sank to the carpet.

He pushed me on my back. I pulled him on top of me, my hips rising to meet him, my thighs trembling. He drove inside me. My legs entwined across his back, my body closing around him. A violence overwhelmed us, our matched movements coming harder, faster. My teeth clenched, grinding until a sharp, hot spear of pleasure shot through me. Above my own scream, I heard Serras's. This time I did not think of death. I did not think at all.

We lay there a long time, our bodies slick with sweat, spent. I thought of all the things I had to do, studying to be done, murders to solve, stress reduction techniques to learn to save my back molars, but still I did not move. My limbs were too heavy; my will too weak. Serras was also still and silent, my head nested on the steady rise and fall of his chest. I suspected him asleep. I lifted my head, ready to awaken him rudely only to meet his heavy-lidded gaze. I stared back at him studying me. I swore softly. He smiled. I rolled off him and sat up, searching for my clothes when his hand closed tight around my rubber-banded wrist. I looked down at him over my shoulder. He looked at me. He had stopped smiling.

"Stay," he said.

I turned away, the long fall of my hair hiding my face. *Sonofabitch*, I thought. My head fell onto my chest. I tasted the scrape of molar against molar. *Sonofabitch*. I sat in a garter belt and thigh-highs on Serras's carpet and cried like a baby.

He made no move until I finished, did not touch me except for his fingers circling my rubber-banded wrist. My tears streamed silently down my face, wetting my bare breasts. Once started, I didn't seem able to stop. My shoulders shook. I drew in heaving gulps of air, swiped at my runny nose, disgusted with myself.

Finally I was able to stop. I shook my head,

still not able to look at Serras. He didn't move as if waiting to make certain I was done. After several seconds with no more display from me than a shoulder twitch and a snuffle or two, he sat up beside me. Holding on to my wrist, he stood, pulling me up with him.

"Sorry," I said without looking at him.

His hand came up to my face. His fingertips brushed away the wetness on my cheeks. "Shut up, Silver," he said softly.

I met his gaze.

"C'mon." He led me down a short, carpeted hallway to a medium-size bedroom and a queen-size bed. "Lie down," he said.

I sat on the mattress's edge, reclined back onto the double pillows. Propped on my elbows, I watched Serras bend over me, remove my garter belt, peel off my stockings. He drew the covers over my naked body, tucked them around me. He leaned over, brushed a kiss on my damp cheek. "Sleep."

When I awoke, dazed and disoriented, it was dark. Serras was gone. I stumbled through the small apartment, switching on lights. On the kitchen table, I found a note. "Be right back."

I stood alone and naked in Serras's kitchenette, totally sated by sex and sleep. I smiled.

"Sonofabitch."

Chapter Eleven

I called a cab, scribbled "Had to go" beneath Serras's note and left the apartment before he returned. On the ride back to Billie's to pick up my car, I avoided thinking about Serras by concentrating on the events of the past weeks. My mind played a montage of the people involved. From a slab, Della stared up at me. She'd called me. Emergency contact. Why?

Paul, too, had made sure I'd pay attention, leaving me everything but the reason why he came to dangle from the rafters. After Paul, came Lucy with her thin body and tough act. I saw Della's picture of her brother in his military uniform, proud, clean shaven and much too young to die such a senseless death. I couldn't envision Ben Herschmann, buried before sundown and suspicion, but I saw his wife, reckless in red, serene on diazepam, married to a man who may have suffered the same fate as her lover. And now free of both.

I was paying the cab driver when my cell phone rang. I handed over the money and grabbed my phone out of my purse as I stepped out of the cab. I pressed Talk.

"Where the hell are you?"

I smiled. "Stop sweet-talking me, Serras."

"I'm gone twenty minutes tops, and you take off on me."

"Don't blame yourself. Men sleep with me once and fall desperately, irrationally, insanely in love with me." I sighed. "It's a cross I bear."

"Silver?" I could hear the smile in his voice.

"Serras?"

"You're scared to death."

I didn't make a sound.

"So scared you'll openly run right into the path of killers but bolt from my bedroom before I get back with a sackful of Chinese and the fixings for breakfast."

"You got Chinese? And went to the grocery store?"

"I figured I had a woman in the house, I'd better take advantage of it and have her make me a hearty breakfast in the morning before she left."

"Here I thought you were worried about me,

but you're just pissed because I won't be frying you up bacon in my thigh-highs and garter belt."

"You really know how to torture a man, Le-Grande."

"I was a well-paid professional at it, Serras."

He laughed low and soft. I thought of the rough heat of his skin, the wonderful gentling of his lips on mine. For a second I regretted not staying warm and stretched out between his sheets.

His laughter died. The silence hung as if something had to be said but neither of us was going to be the one to say it.

"I—"

"You—"

We both started speaking at the same time, then shut down as soon as we heard the other. One more beat of silence.

"Serras?"

"Yeah?"

"We're pathetic."

"Yeah."

"So, you going to ask me to sleep with you again?"

"I don't remember having to ask you this time."

I laughed softly.

"Say I do ask, what are you going to answer?"

I was smiling. Snap out of it, I told myself. But to Serras I said, "First, you've got to ask."

"I'll ask," he said, the low promise in his voice buckling my knees. "Good night, Silver."

The line went dead. The man may not have been a professional but he had a few class-A torture techniques of his own.

I had walked to my car and slouched against its side as I talked to Serras. I clicked off my phone and slid up straight. I had found my keys and unlocked the car when two shadows at the far end of the parking lot caught my attention.

It was not late by club standards. The parking lot was full, the lights of cars coming and going sweeping across the open paved square, the noise and music inside spilling out into the night. Any sobriety spurred by Paul's service today had been as brief as his own occasional attempts at restraint. By this hour, when inhibitions have dissolved and decorum is ridiculed, there is little reason to hide.

I peered into the darkness concealing the two figures. A car started, pulled out, its brief illumination at the far end of the lot causing the figures to step back. But not before I saw a flash of scarlet, a woman's shapely form. I didn't remember seeing Fiona at Billie's after Paul's funeral. If she hadn't come then, what would bring her here at this late hour? Had she come certain her country club comrades were many miles and social stratums away? Or had someone else arranged the meeting? Who was the other figure? One of Billie's regulars? One of Billie's friends?

I locked the car, started toward the darkness. I crouched down, weaving my way through the rows of parked cars, stopping when a car entered or left until lights swept above me. By the time I reached the side of the building, the two figures had moved to the alleyway that led to the back entrance and Billie's office. I flattened myself against the building's side.

"I like getting screwed literally," a man snarled. I didn't recognize the voice. "Not figuratively."

"Well, at least, I this time someone else gets enjoyment."

Even more unexpected than Fiona Herschmann's well-modulated tones was the crack of a hard slap, a thud as something hit the wall right angle to the one my own suddenly nonbreathing body pressed against. I imagined Fiona's well-shaped head snapping back, slamming against the solid surface and still not a hair of her elegant updo coming loose.

"Temper, temper," Fiona chided, the disdain in her voice daring the man to raise a hand to her again, the taunting subtly indicating an undertone of pleasure. "It's your kind's own lack of control that got us all into this mess."

"Certainly you're not unfamiliar with the pleasures of excess, Mrs. Herschmann. Or is screwing anything not nailed down what passes for restraint in your set these days?"

"Is choking as a form of postcoital intimacy what passes for restraint in your set these days?"

I flinched as I heard another hard slap, a thump against the wall. Was a bit of knockabout Fiona's idea of foreplay? And what had she meant by that last remark? Was Della's killer only around the corner? I pressed myself against the wall, a sensation of standing in the center of a runaway elevator taking hold.

"Ask your husband. And Figuero's people. He was the one in bed with them. At least he made it easy for us," the man said with a viciousness much more cutting than any physical force. "We didn't have to lift a finger."

"Fate does take a hand sometimes, doesn't it?"

"Tell me—" the man's voice turned intimate "—was he wearing the heels when you found him?"

The profanity Fiona called the man sounded strangely complimentary in her elegant tone.

"Temper, temper," the man mocked.

"Are we done?" Fiona demanded. "Anyone who could have hurt us is dead now."

"Including Ben," the man noted.

"So, it's over. There's no one left."

"Except you."

"As you've pointed out, I have many hungers, but among them is not the wish to harm you...or anyone else."

"Unless something happens to you," the man qualified, as if this line of conversation had taken place before.

"We both agree I am known for my animal instincts. Survival is among them."

"I say you're bluffing. You've got nothing and never did."

Fiona's voice turned to the low, seductive tones of a born siren. "Are you willing to find out?"

I heard silence and smiled. She had him by the apricots, and everyone involved in the conversation was well aware of it.

"What about your dead lover's ex-wife."

I flattened myself farther against the wall.

"I don't think she knows anything about it."

From my secret spot, I sent Fiona the thumbs up sign.

"She was with Paul the last night of his life."

"But she wasn't the last person with him."

I heard the satisfaction in Fiona's tone.

"Neither were you, darling," the man reminded her.

"I wouldn't boast. Your man almost got taken out with a piece of costume jewelry." Fiona's soft laughter drifted into the night.

"She's lucky he didn't kill her for that alone."

This was the creep who'd sicked the bigger creep on me? Oh, yeah, moron, I thought. Your bullet-headed muscleman was lucky I hadn't been wearing Adrienne's spiked dog collar.

"You can't touch her," Fiona goaded. "Not with that good-looking cop hovering around her all the time."

I smiled, despite everything, still having to proclaim a fondness for Fiona.

"Don't worry about Serras. I know how to handle him. You do your job. I'll do mine. And everybody will live happily ever after."

Except for the four people all ready dead, I thought.

I heard steps moving away from me. I slid against the building, working my way to the corner. I gripped the wall's edge, revealing as little of myself as possible as I curved around the corner. I caught Fiona and her partner-in-crime's backsides slipping into Billie's back entrance. The man wore a suit, was shorter, slighter than his henchman I'd met the other night. His hair, its color indecipherable in the dim light as they moved inside was cropped close to the head, cutting a strong line across his nape. He didn't look like a murderer or even someone who would have a hardworking, community college coed, part-time limo driver, ex-stripper throttled.

The back door closed. I breathed for the first time in several seconds. I had to get inside the club, see the man's face. I turned and ran head-first into a solid mass.

I flew back, hit the ground hard. One hand was in my purse, already closing around my .32 when I saw it was Sweet Sam standing above me. He stretched out his hand to me.

"Goodness, Miss Silver, I saw someone sneaking around the building and feared we were in for some more trouble. Here I see it's you slipping around like the Devil's dead. You could get yourself hurt out here all alone this time of night. Not safe for a young woman such as yourself." He shook his head, highly distressed.

"C'mon on, now, Sweet Sam. You know you don't have to worry about me. Wasn't so long ago I left here every night at unlawful hours and lived to tell the tales." I took his offered hand. He lifted me as if gravity hadn't been invented.

"Don't matter," Sam said, inconsolable. "Still not safe. Not safe at all."

"Why isn't it safe, darlin?'"

He looked away from me. His hands made nervous wringing movements.

"What did you mean, Sam, when you said you feared 'we were in for some more trouble?' Has there been trouble around Billie's recently? Something you saw that wasn't good?"

"I gots to get back in now, Miss Silver. Miss Billie has gone home for the night, and she'll give me a good what-for if she finds out I let the glasses pile up and the limes run out."

"Sure, Sam." I took his arm, moved by the blatant distress on his face. "I was just on my way in myself, but I much prefer arriving on the arm of a handsome escort." We started in toward the kitchen. "You say Miss Billie has gone home?"

"She gots the head pain that likes to lay her low."

As we reached the kitchen doorway that looked into the main room, I searched for Fiona and her friend. "Did she say anyone could use her office?" I asked, wondering if they had slipped in there.

"Miss Billie don't let anyone in her office.

You coming back to Billie's, Miss Silver." The dread had disappeared from Sam's face. His teeth showed white as he smiled.

"Just visiting."

"I miss you, Miss Silver."

I reached up on tiptoe to buss his cheek. "I miss you, Sweet Sam. You stay safe now, and don't let Miss Billie boss you around."

As I left him at the doorway, I wondered behind his wide grin, what had he seen? What did he know that even the suggestion made his expression fill with fear?

I made my way through the main room. Business was good for a weeknight. A new girl in top hat and thong was onstage. I searched the crowd, still looking for Fiona and her slap-happy friend. I saw nothing. I made my way toward the ladies' room, turned the opposite way down the hall to Billie's office. Checking to make sure no one else was around, I pressed my ear to the office door. I heard nothing. I slowly twisted the doorknob. The office was locked. No light showed beneath the door. I listened a few seconds longer, turned and headed back toward the main room. Fiona and her mystery man must have left right after their meeting. I went to the bar, slid onto a seat and swiveled toward the crowd.

"What it'll be?"

I swiveled back to a statuesque blonde as she automatically slapped a cocktail napkin down in front of me.

"Virgin Mary," I said, punctuated with a hearty snap of my elastic.

She smiled, showing white, straight teeth, before she sauntered off. The smooth slant of her cheekbones and her wide eyes that spoke of an innocence long gone reminded me of Della. I didn't remember seeing the bartender at her colleague's funeral service.

"You work here long?" I asked when she returned with my drink.

"Long enough," she said, still smiling, but a blankness in her expression told me when she was young, this is not the way she had pictured her life.

"I used to work here myself." I picked up the celery stalk, took a large chomp.

"Yeah?" Her interest was minimal.

"I was a dancer. Left about a year ago."

"That right?"

"I go to community college," I persisted as if I were a role model.

"I'm working on my doctoral dissertation on Translucent Identities–The Legal Metamorphoses in the Genetic Era." Bored, she started to move away.

"You know Della Devine?"

She stopped. I might have imagined it, my tendency toward suspicion lately multiplied by recent events, but I thought I detected tenseness in the woman's stance. First Sweet Sam, now Blondie the Bartender. What was going on at Billie's? Had I been way off from the beginning, nosing around the Oyster Club?

The blonde turned to me. "I knew of her. She'd moved on before I started here."

I stirred my tomato juice with the celery stalk, met the blonde's gaze. "So you know what happened to her?"

The blonde crossed her arms across her ample chest. "Yeah, I know what happened to her. Everyone who works here knows the story."

"Heard any theories on who killed her?"

I watched the blonde's gaze shift about the room, confirming she knew something about Della's death.

"She was my friend," I told her when she didn't answer.

She shrugged. "People talk, you know."

"What do they say?"

"They say she went a little crazy after her brother's death. Starting talking nonsense."

"What kind of nonsense."

"That she was the reason for his death."

"How'd she figure that?"

"According to Della, her brother was anti-drug big time on account of all her problems. Supposedly he'd learned of a drug operation right on the base."

"People buying and selling?"

"A little, but mainly transporting."

"Transporting?"

"Cargo planes. Military operations carrying cases of the stuff sailing across international lines. All sanctioned by Uncle Sam. According to Della, her brother went to some brass with proof. A week later he was run down by a train. Della said they killed him."

"What did the other girls say?"

"The crack had made her paranoid, had her spouting off conspiracy theories."

"What do you think?"

The blonde shrugged. "I'm not paid to think. I'm paid to pour drinks." She moved off to tend to other customers. I chomped down on my celery and chewed thoughtfully as I swiveled toward the floor, searching in vain for a blonde in scarlet and her well-dressed escort. I saw nothing. I turned back to the bar to leave a bigger-than-usual tip for the blonde. She was drawing a draft not far down the bar.

"The base where Della's brother was stationed?" I asked.

She flipped her long hair over her shoulder to look at me.

"The men there used to be steady customers when I was here. They still come in regularly?"

She finished off the beer with a neat inch of foam and delivered it to the customer. Wiping her hands on a towel, she came back toward me, glanced down at the twenty I'd left on the bar.

"Like clockwork," she answered my question.

"Any of them ever talk about Della's brother's death?"

Her gaze flitted around the room, came back to center on me. "Two came in one night. They were pretty drunk. It was a slow night, quiet. I'd heard the stories from a couple of the girls and was curious."

"So you asked them?"

She nodded.

"What did they say?"

"At first they looked at each other, and I didn't think they were going to say anything. But then this Latino-looking fellow, he was the drunker of the two, he says rules are made so people don't get hurt. People break the rules, accidents happen. I asked him if Della's brother broke the rules?"

"What'd he say?"

"Nothing. The Latino's friend moved in, told him to shut his trap and me to bring the booze and mind my own business." The blonde picked up the twenty, folded it, slipped it into her bra. "That's when I started thinking maybe Della wasn't so crazy as everybody said. Next thing I hear she's dead in an alleyway."

And since then, three more. As the blonde walked away, I decided she was right. Maybe Della wasn't as crazy as everybody said.

Auntie was up when I got home watching reruns of *Sex and the City* and drinking wheatgrass tonic. She watched me as I slipped off my shoes, plopped down in an armchair and rifled through the ever-growing pile of mail.

"Adrienne home?" I looked up, meeting her expectant gaze.

"Hours ago. She's studying in her room."

Guilt fell on me as I realized I would be wise to follow her example. I had popped in my tape of recited notes into the car's cassettes player, listening to them as I drove between destinations. Still my mind had been elsewhere. My retention level nil. I glanced at the television screen, back at Auntie with her waiting expression. She had been watching me since I came in. A tiny closemouthed smile tweaked the corners of her mouth.

"Nice service today."

I nodded.

"You left rather abruptly."

"Sometimes it's better not to fight the tide."

"Amen," Auntie muttered.

We stared at the television screen in silence for a few minutes, my gaze on the picture but my thoughts elsewhere. Auntie absently hummed "She'll Be Coming around the Mountain."

"That friend of Adrienne's father." Auntie abruptly broke off her humming but kept her eyes on the television screen. "The one who just passed away."

"Ben Herschmann?" I supplied.

Auntie nodded. "He was found hanging off the closet door."

"How did you find that out?"

The tiny smile reappeared. "I have my inside sources."

She took a swig of wheatgrass. I thought of Wilson Bintliff with his shiny shoes and satin-lined caskets and secretive, close-mouthed smile turned several times that day toward Auntie. Death does make strange bedfellows.

"So you and Wilson had a 'chat'?"

Auntie nodded.

"Seems he's good friends with the fella who handled the Herschmann service."

"Was Ben Herschmann's death voluntary or involuntary?"

Auntie set down her wheatgrass, looked at me. "I'm good, Silver, but I'm not that good."

"Tonight when I went back to Billie's to get my car, I saw the merry widow chitchatting with someone at the back entrance to the club." I told Auntie what I'd heard between Fiona and her friend, their abrupt disappearance. Then I relayed my conversation with the bartender.

Auntie switched off the television. "So Fiona Herschmann was married to Bennie, sleeping with Paul, and two out of three of the triangle are dead?"

"Her lover murdered and made to look like a suicide. Her husband a suspected suicide made to look like a natural death. And Fiona daring someone to do the same to her and suffer the nasty consequences."

"You think she's straight-up or just smart?"

Both, I was secretly hoping. I shook my head.

"You said Fiona told you Paul had come on to her at her husband's request, to see if she was having him followed?" Auntie asked.

I nodded.

"Her husband must have been up to some shenanigans or he wouldn't have worried if his wife was having him watched. If Bennie had been a saint, Fiona would have come up empty-handed. So Bennie must have had some hobbies that had him sweating bullets."

"Obviously some other people knew about these hobbies. People that Fiona said could hurt Ben," I added. "She told me she fell in love with Paul."

Auntie shrugged. "Didn't most women?"

"If she became emotionally involved…" I rubbed my forehead. It'd been a long day. My thoughts were blurring. My talk was rambling. I stood up, frustrated and tired. "I need to get a good night's sleep. Maybe all this will make sense in the morning when my head is clear."

"Yes, you've put in a full day," Auntie said with her niggling smile.

I shot her the same smile back. "You, too. Good night all."

"Silver," Auntie stopped me at the doorway to the hall. I glanced back at her. "I like that detective."

The hell of it was, I thought as I continued toward my bedroom, so did I.

I woke in the morning and cursed the hour. I turned on to my side, positioning my face to where the sun slanted across my pillow. The heat on my skin and the promise of light past the thin shield of my eyelids was enough to make me believe the answer to the question of who killed Della, Paul, Lucy, perhaps even Ben Herschmann, would come. But not in the next ten minutes I spent lying there, reviewing the images and events in my mind. I rolled onto my back, out of the sun and propped myself up, reaching for the textbook that, like me, had survived my latest wild ride a few nights ago.

I opened to the chapter I should have read several days ago, the pages already loosening from their binding. As I reached for the micro-cassette recorder to recite my notes, the book slipped from my lap to the carpet. Groaning, I leaned over as far as possible without tumbling off the edge of the mattress and grasped the book's broken spine. The pages fluttered as I lifted the book. From between them, a round circle fell, rolled onto the carpet.

Leaning over again, I grabbed it. It was a cardboard coaster, the disposable kind offered generously to bars with free advertising and cute sayings designed to capture patrons' attentions. I stared at the coaster with a beer brand printed on one side. The day I'd gone to the Oyster, the bartender had set the same kind of coaster beneath my ginger ale. This one could be from the Oyster. Or it could be one from any bar within a one-hundred-mile radius that sold the same brand of beer and had been visited by a sales rep in the last month bearing freebies. The question was, what was it doing tucked between the pages of my textbook?

Beneath the beer ad, there was a trivia question. I guessed at the answer, turned the coaster over to see if I was right. Written in slightly smeared heavy black was my answer. A telephone number. Beneath the number a name. All caps. I stared hard until the end letter reversed itself.

Doyle.

I ran my index finger over the dark lines like a blind person reading Braille. The color came off on my fingertips. I was guessing eyeliner pencil. I glanced at the textbook with its flattened cover. I stared again at the name, the numbers, my index finger hovering above the lines almost lovingly now. Had Lucy, after all, told me something?

I threw back the sheet, swung my legs over the edge of the bed, noted I needed a major waxing, and stood, coaster held gingerly in my sweaty palm to avoid smearing the writing on it anymore. I put it on the dresser as I opened the top drawer and got my daily dose of rubber band. I showered, dressed, copied the name and number onto the back of an old clothing receipt, careful not to transpose the numbers. I slipped the coaster into my denim shorts' side pocket, tucked the inked receipt into my rear pocket and tripped down the staircase.

Auntie was coming in, flushed from her kickboxing class when I reached the kitchen. Adrienne, bless her heart, was grating potatoes for knishes. I opened the cupboard over the Faberware percolator, grabbed a monster-size insulated cup, slammed the door with more excitement than my usual early-morning irritation and filled my mini-thermos to the brim with French roast. As I reached for the half 'n half, I saw Auntie and Adrienne exchanging glances.

"What?" I asked more out of fun than irritation. They both had lived with me long enough to know not to speak to me until after thirty-two ounces of caffeine. Did they think sleeping with Serras once was going to make me the Kelly Ripka of midmorning Memphis? Even if I was feeling particularly jaunty this a.m., I'd be damned if I'd let them know.

"Before kickboxing, I was looking at that Tae Bo ad. You know, the one with the handsome black man," Auntie was telling Adrienne, having lived with me long enough to ignore me until noon.

"Billie Blanks," Adrienne supplied, also having lived with me long enough.

"That's the one. And I was thinking I should shave my head."

I sipped my coffee and smiled inwardly, happy. I might have mentioned it before but it bears repeating. I love my auntie.

"What do you think, Adrienne?" Auntie requested opinions.

Adrienne frowned down at her grated potato, the clear, sticky juice running down her forearm to elbow. "You've got to begin gradually," she said, her voice weighty as if she had pondered the subject long and hard. "Before going bald, you should begin with a tattoo, then pierce a few body parts." She turned to Auntie, her eyes earnest behind the wire-rim glasses she only wore early morning and late night while her contact lenses were soaking. "Only then, you shave your head."

"Adrienne's right," I concurred. "Got to give it a few good nights' sleep before you shave the skull."

Auntie slipped off her Nike headband. "Just a whim anyway. But think of the freedom. Get up, spray a little Pledge on the head and be off." She studied me as she patted her cheeks with the ends of the towel around her neck.

"You're unusually social this morning." I saw the knowing glance she sent Adrienne.

Too excited to be irritated, I picked up my coffee lifeline. "Got to go, guys."

"Whoa. I'm making knishes," Adrienne protested.

I patted her cheek as I passed. "I'll be back before they're browned. I've just got to make a call."

"And there's no phone here?" Auntie asked.

"Caller ID," I reasoned.

Auntie's and Adrienne's eyes both narrowed like two doms dividing territories.

"So, no one has a cell phone?" Auntie levied.

But I was already out the door. One-half mile and two sharp turns away, I was at a pay phone outside a minimart. I deposited the change, dialed the number, listened to three rings. Four rings. Five rings.

I was becoming disheartened when I heard a click, then nothing. Whoever was on the other end stopped breathing.

"Doyle?"

Chapter Twelve

Nothing.

"Doyle," I insisted again, congratulating myself even for my calm tone as I spoke the syllable.

"Who's calling?" The voice was deep male with a jagged rasp as if its owner had been chewing glass.

"Della," I said. "Della Devine."

The line went dead.

I hung up and leaned against the half-glass booth, feeling the satisfaction of a day's work already done. The phone rang. Doyle had reversed the call. I picked up.

"Devine," I said, feeling every ounce.

"Who the hell is this?" the flinty voice demanded at the other end.

I closed my eyes and leaned, letting the Plexiglas support my body as it sagged with the satisfaction. Finally a break. "Who the hell is this? Doyle?"

"That's not important."

"It is to me. And to a few other people. Paul Chumsky, Lucy Champlain, Ben Herschmann."

Another silence, then the sandpaper voice asked, "What've you got?"

"What you want."

"How the hell do you know what I want?"

I didn't, but my motto has always been if you can't make it, fake it. Rarely could anyone tell the difference.

"It's a talent of mine." A good stripper zeroes in on peoples' desires. A bad stripper uses them against them. Had Della become a bad stripper? "Seems it's a talent of some other people, too." My voice turned coaxing. "They know what you need. Maybe even better than you do. Is that what happened to you, Doyle? Did someone else know what you needed?"

I heard a mean chuckle. The other line had the hollow, echoing reception that told me Doyle was on a cell phone. "You just tell me what you're going to give me."

It was not the voice that had whispered sweet nothings in my ear in the Luxury Limo parking lot. Nor was it the voice that had been chatting with Fiona last night in between rearranging her jawline.

"It's a two-way street, Doyle."

"What do you want—" he paused for emphasis before he said "—Silver?"

My first impulse was to slam down the phone and run back to the sweet sanctity of my 200-thread-count sheets and sun-slanted pillow. I curled the telephone cord around my wrist like my rubber band and gave a good tug.

"Answers." I didn't deny the identity. He knew who I was. I'd have been a little disappointed if he hadn't.

"And what do I get?"

"You get what you killed Della and the others for."

"That's an ugly accusation, Silver."

"Murder isn't exactly pretty."

"Your friends are dead, Silver. So if I wanted something from them, I'd already have it."

"Then why are people still dying, Doyle?"

His low, cold laugh came again over the line. "Fact of life, Silver." He said my name with an intimacy that made a bead of sweat roll down my spine. "People die."

I straightened. "If you're going to insult me, Doyle, I'm hanging up now."

"Just when it was getting interesting?" he taunted.

"How's this for interesting?" I tried to keep my voice controlled, but my mind raced, trying to process all the events of the past week and form a connection. I flashbacked to that night in the side street next to Luxury Limousines, the bully breathing in my ear. *Where is it? Where is it?* I smiled. "Maybe you've gotten rid of anyone who can cause you trouble—

"Except you."

"Don't interrupt me, Doyle," I said sourly. "Della, Paul, Lucy, even Ben, although the jury's out if you'll receive bonus points for that one. They've all been eliminated. All that killing, and you still aren't sure. You took Della out because she was expendable from the start, Paul because maybe he knew more than he should, at the very least, his death could conveniently close the case. But you're still breaking out in a cold sweat, so you double your bets with Lucy, probably Ben. Still you go to bed at night, lay your greasy little head on that soft pillow, stare up at the ceiling and you know."

I waited.

"What do I know, sweetheart?" Sarcasm filled his flinty voice.

"It's still out there."

It was a big chance, a stab in the dark. If I was wrong, Doyle would know I'd been bluffing all along and the conversation was over. But if the instincts I'd learned to rely on at a young age were right, here was the opportunity to make Doyle squirm. He didn't answer. Bingo. I had mine.

"Della and Paul were amateurs, way out of their league, but both had been around long enough to know you don't trust anyone." I paused.

"Please continue," Doyle said with an oily graciousness that made my toenails peel.

"Maybe somebody got greedy. After all, country club pros don't have half-million-dollar bank accounts from teaching broads how to birdie. Maybe someone threatened to tell if they didn't get what they wanted? Maybe Della and Paul were partners, but then somebody decided to negotiate their own deal? Maybe Della demanded more and was killed as a warning to Paul to stop playing around? Enough persuasion. Paul says he's done, but Paul wasn't stupid. He saw what you did to Della, knew he was next. He hands over what got this whole party started in the first place. You put him out of his misery. End of story."

Doyle said nothing. I had him on the ropes.

Except for one thing you didn't know about my ex-husband." I thought of Fiona's conversation with the mystery man last night. *I like getting screwed...literally not figuratively.*

"Paul loved to get the last laugh."

No response. TKO.

"So you killed Della, then Paul, setting up Paul to take the rap for Della's death. Both principals are out of the picture, the cops close a quick lid on the case because whoever wanted what Della and Paul had probably has influence. Hell, it could have been the commissioner himself salivating over their bodies."

An amused laugh that set my back molars in motion came from the other end. I said nothing, hoping my caller would fill in the blanks.

The laugh died away. "Don't stop now, Silver. It's just getting interesting. We must be coming to the good part? Tell me how the bad guy gets caught and the good guy rides away with the girl into the sunset, and all's right once again in this big, bad crazy world."

"The ending is up to you, Doyle."

"How generous. Let me make sure I have this correct. Della and Paul had something I wanted very badly."

"Still want badly," I reinforced.

"According to your version. Badly enough I would kill. Della decided to make her own deal and upped the ante. She was made an example of to anyone else, say Paul, thinking of getting demanding. Fortunately, Paul has a sudden change of heart, only to end up strung up like a trophy-winning marlin in his Fruit of the Looms. Not a very dignified way to go, I'm afraid, but he did see it coming and made provisions to best the best."

A beat of silence passed. I waited for Doyle to make the move.

"I only have one question."

Inside my head I heard the sound of my teeth scraping.

"Tell me what it is I want?"

Busted.

"You refer again and again throughout your entertaining anecdote to the mysterious thing that can bring a man to his knees or to murder. I'm anxious to know. What is it?"

Of course, I'd made it up as I went, my heart racing and my teeth grating, the connections in my mind coming fast and furious. Now I waited for the spurt of adrenaline that would give me the answer.

The voice turned mean. "Answer the question."

When I was born, the doctor had decided to use forceps. According to my mother, I'd taken a peek from between her thighs, seen a man with a mask coming toward me with metal thongs and slipped back in. I was born Cesarean. I don't know how much of the story is truth and how much is labor drug-induced fiction. What I do know is in the thirty-two years since, I hadn't let a man use metal devices on or me or order me around…although many have tried both.

"Answer my question," I told Doyle. "Who killed Della, Paul, Lucy and why? How is Ben Herschmann involved in all this?"

"Give it up, sweetheart. You've got nothing and you know it."

I did know it. Now Doyle knew it, too. Still I wasn't ready to hang up. I took a cue from Fiona, made my voice honey. "Are you willing to find out?"

Doyle's watery laugh came across the wire again. "Serras was right about you, sweetheart."

I heard the silence after a shot is fired.

"Who's bluffing now, Doyle?"

"Are you willing to find out?"

When I didn't response, he said, "People believe what they want to believe. Remember that."

"Another fact of life?" I mocked.

His voice changed from eerily pleasant to cold steel. "Since you're a friend of Serras's, I'll give you a piece of advice. You're way out of your element, little girl. Just like your dead friends."

I was composing my comeback when static cut across the line. The connection had been cut. I replaced the receiver, waited to see if it would ring again. After a few minutes I headed to my car and drove home. The knishes were still warm in a covered pan on the stove, but I had no appetite. I went for a second thirty-two ounces of caffeine and sat down at the table.

"So?" Auntie was at the table, the morning edition folded at her elbow. She aimed at me the gaze that said her patience was coming to an end. Next to her, Adrienne sat, a fleck of potato pancake on her chin and her expression sympathetic.

I looked past them, sipped my coffee and considered Serras. I was scared, not because I had slept with him but because I had trusted him. A toe-curling orgasm could forgive a multitude of flaws, but being made a fool of made women like Lorena Bobbitt folk heroes.

"Silver?" Auntie's concerned voice brought my thoughts back from a scenario involving Serras and a weed whacker.

"What's the matter?"

I pulled out the coaster, set it on the tabletop.

"Doyle?" Adrienne read, peering at the cardboard circle through her wire rims. She looked up at me. "Who's that?"

I reached over, brushed the crumb from her chin.

"It's the last person Della called the night she was murdered. Lucy overheard her make arrangements to meet. This morning I found this between the pages of the textbook I had in the limo the night I drove Lucy home." I tapped the coaster. "Lucy must have stuck it in there."

"How'd Lucy get the name and number?" Auntie asked.

"I don't know. Maybe she picked the phone out of the trash, brought up the last number dialed. Maybe she was in on it from the beginning. Maybe she worked for Doyle, saw what happened to Della and Paul and was afraid she might be next. Maybe no one had ever offered her a ride home in a white limousine before. All I know is this morning I found that name and number."

"Who's Doyle?" Adrienne asked again.

"I don't know."

"So you called the number?" Auntie said.

I nodded. "To find out."

"Did you?"

"Not yet." I relayed the conversation. Adrienne listened, her lips parted and her gaze never leaving me. Auntie alternated which brow to lift.

"There's one more thing," I said when I finished. "He knows Serras."

Understanding came into Auntie's eyes followed by compassion. I looked away from her.

"That docsn't mean—"

"Don't," I warned her. I pushed away from the table and stood. "I've got class in forty-five minutes, and the traffic is hell this time of day." I headed toward the stairs. I was up on the second landing before they began to discuss the situation in low tones.

After class, I ignored the rare light breeze attempting to make the heat bearable and headed to the cramped, airless library, determined to revive my flailing academic career. I took a seat in a narrow cubby behind the rows of books, away from the windows, got out my Info Processing Fundamentals, Sixth Edition, a notebook, pen and prepared to do battle.

I opened to chapter eleven. I glanced at the syllabus I'd taped to the notebook's inside cover. I was behind five chapters. I rcad the chapter title, began to read the first paragraph, the tip of my index finger underlining the text, guiding my gaze, my lips silently mouthing the words. Still the letters became backward, forcing me to slow down, focus harder. By the end of the paragraph, I could feel the headache beginning and my frustration rising. I reached for my wrist but found only skin and bone. I looked down and saw I'd forgotten to slip on a rubber band.

I rubbed my naked wrist and forced myself back to the text, fighting the urge to drop my head and bang my forehead repeatedly against the pages. Ten pages later I lost the fight. A good five-minute bout of head banging made me feel like a new woman. I slammed the book closed, slipped everything into my wide-strapped carrier and, with a curious calm, walked out of the library.

I paused outside the entrance next to a square trashcan and stared down at the garbage. I slipped off my book bag, unzipped it and turning it upside down, dumped its contents into the trash container. When it was empty, I threw the carrier on top of the books, notepads, Papermate pens and other tools of my short-lived student career.

I walked to my car with no weight on my shoulders. I pulled out my cell phone, speed dialed Luxury Limousines. I hadn't had a gig since the night I took Lucy home, which normally wouldn't worry me except this was prime-time wedding season, and I was usually booked every weekend. The dispatcher picked up, said no, nothing not already assigned in the next few weeks, but they'd call me if something came up and they needed a driver. Considering my recent refusals to cooperate, I suspected Vito Figuero had sent word I was not exactly employee-of-the-month material.

I got in my car. There were other limo companies. Vito Figuero couldn't have all of them in his back pocket. I exited left off the campus onto the main road. I stopped at a gas station for a full tank and a cherry Slush Puppie. I was coming out the minimart door, slipping on my sunglasses and about to enjoy my first sip when I saw the dark coupe idling in the parking space next to mine. Serras leaned against the side of the car, chewing gum and taking me in from behind mirrored lenses.

"What?" I snapped, letting him know right from the start the fun and games were finished. "It's illegal to sell Slush Puppies before noon?"

"No," he said, unsmiling. "Just to drink one." He cracked his gum.

I wrapped my lips around the straw and took

a long sip that sucked my cheeks into a fish face. "You stalking me, Serras?"

"I was pulling into the campus when I saw you leaving."

"What do you want?"

"It's almost eleven-thirty, LeGrande. Shouldn't you be at least civil by now?"

I finished off another long slurp. "I was actually in a pretty good mood this morning, Serras."

He cocked his head. I saw myself in his reflective lenses. The sunglasses stayed steady on me, but I knew behind them, Serras scanned the area. "What happened? You woke up?"

"I had an interesting phone conversation with a man named Doyle."

I sensed Serras's gaze on me now. "Care to share?"

I got out the coaster I'd slipped into my purse, handed it to Serras.

He took in the name and number, turned the coaster over, then over again. "Where did this come from?"

"Lucy. She left it between the pages of a textbook I had in the car the night I gave her a ride home from the Oyster. The night before she was murdered."

"Who's Doyle?"

"The man Della called the night before she was murdered. Remember Lucy told me she had seen the phone Della had used in the trash later that night. She must have picked it up, checked to see if it was still working, saw the last call made. Maybe the cleaning lady saw the phone in the trash, picked it up, set it aside in case one of the girls came looking for it. Lucy came in the next day, worked the first shift." I paused. "Maybe Lucy was in on it from the beginning. Maybe she knew who killed Della and why and took it to her grave before she had a chance to tell anyone."

Serras studied the coaster.

"I called the number."

His gaze came up.

"This morning." I relayed the conversation. Serras leaned against the car and said nothing.

"One more fun fact."

Serras waited. My Slush Puppie was melting. I reached up, slid the mirrored lenses off his face. His gaze remained concealed.

"Doyle claims to know you."

Serras's expression didn't change.

"We were talking, and I was being my usual wit on a stick when Doyle comes back with 'Serras was right about you.'"

"And?"

"I told him he was bluffing. He said, 'People believe what they want to believe.'"

"What do you believe, Silver?"

I looked up into that face of hard lines and even stronger sensuality. "I know I don't like being played for a fool."

His expression had stayed maddeningly inscrutable throughout the conversation. It did not change now. "Is that what you think this is all about."

The Slush Puppie was sweating on the plastic cup's outside. Moisture trickled down my forearm. "Could be part of it. Somebody thought I might have what everyone is looking for. I don't see why you wouldn't wonder about it, too."

"I do."

My grip tightened around the plastic Slush Puppie cup.

"And you think that's why I slept with you? Hoping the truth would come out over pillow talk?"

"Why did you sleep with me, Serras?"

He reached for his sunglasses. I gave them back to him. He slipped them on his face. "Because, Silver, you never sold yourself short."

He did not look at me again. I watched him get in the coupe and pull away. I walked over to the trashcan, dropped the half-finished Slush Puppie into it and walked to my car. I had been made a fool, but not by Serras. I had accomplished the task all by myself.

No cars were in the drive when I got home. The house with its welcoming porch and window boxes failed to bring me the usual sense of calm and constancy I now craved. I parked, went into the kitchen, up the stairs, returned with a thick heavy-duty elastic around my wrist and the morning edition grabbed from the wicker basket in the hall. I poured myself a glass of sweet tea and went out onto the front porch.

I settled into a rocker, set my tea on the table beside me and opened to the classifieds. The porch overhang gave shade but no other relief from the heat. I stared at the newsprint, the headache from this morning moving in around my frontal lobes. My powers of concentration were zero. I folded the paper, dropped it onto the floor next to the chair, took a long drink of tea. Not much call for ex-strippers fresh out of academic probation these days, anyway.

I pressed the glass to my forehead, rolled it across my brow. My hair was twisted up tight. Still, loose strands stuck to the nape of my neck. I smelled of sweat and tasted of Slush

Puppie. I stood, picked up the paper to pore over later and went inside to draw a cool bath.

I stretched out as much as possible in the bath. My knees popped up like pointy twin peaks through the jasmine-scented bubbles. I slathered cucumber-avocado cleansing masque on my face, leaned back and rested my head against the tub, waiting for the masque and the cool water and the scent of the South in the springtime to do its magic. My mind drifted, returning always to the events of the past week and the questions surrounding them. My mind paraded pictures of each of the victims, each of the players. Except one. Ben Herschmann.

I reached over the side of the tub for the bucket of floating plastic ducks in primary colors. Floating ducks had been used to lure me into the tub as a child and had kept me there until the bathwater went cold and my skin shriveled. Nowadays the bright sight of them in the bucket beside the tub made me smile every time I stepped into the bathroom, a fact that I suspected played no small part in my healthy constitution.

I dumped the bucket into the water. The ducks righted themselves, bobbed about the small waves. I selected a pink one, set it on the tub's wide edge. "Della," I said. Beside the pink ducky, I placed a light blue one. "Paul." On the other side, a yellow one. "Lucy."

I continued until each of the primary individuals involved had a duck namesake. Ben Herschmann was white; Fiona was red, Serras dark blue. Then I began to put them in the water, grouping and regrouping them according to the information I had. Della knew Paul and Lucy. Did Lucy know Paul? Maybe some of the other dancers at the Oyster would know. Paul knew Ben Herschmann and the fetching Fiona. Did Ben and his bride know anyone at the Oyster? Fiona had rendezvoused with a man at Billie's. Coincidence or another Auntie Peggilee snort? Either way, I had to add another duck for Fiona's friend who had ordered the monster— hopefully now one-eyed, courtesy of *moi* and Auntie's chandelier earrings—to rearrange my vocal cords. Another duck.

I slid a black duck into the water. Doyle. He could be connected to Della definitely, Lucy maybe and supposedly Serras. I pushed the duck down under the water but it bounced back up, grinning.

"Haven't you ever heard of a 'dead duck,' Doyle?" I asked the plastic toy.

I picked up the last duck. A purple one. Billie. I dropped it into the middle of the others.

Della had worked for Billie. As had I. Billie knew Paul, Serras, possibly Fiona. Sweet Sam's voice played in my memory. "I just don't want no more trouble, Miss Silver."

I stood, sending the ducks bobbing madly in the bath water. I reached for a towel, rubbed my body dry, slipped on a stretch halter and capris, twisted my hair back up, chose a pair of Auntie's shoulder duster earrings from her stash because a girl can never be too careful.

The manager of the Meadows had generously offered to box up Paul's desk and locker and send everything over along with Paul's last check, but I had said I preferred to do it myself. I knew the chances were slim I'd find anything. The police had said they'd searched the house, car, Paul's office, but the quick work made of the case made me doubt their thoroughness. I myself had gone through the house several times on the pretense of cleaning, sorting, preparing to put the house on the market. The car also. And found nothing. The only place I hadn't looked was the office.

I checked the time. The country club early-morning hardcores would be home already or at the horseshoe bar in the clubhouse. Either way, they would all be long gone. The lunch crowd would have joined them at the bar's brass rail or were sunning or steaming themselves somewhere on the premises. It was that restless, lush time of midday when those either retired or rich enough not to work grew prone to conversation and speculation. Not so in the early morning when the day is fresh and possibilities endless nor at dinner hour with its rituals and formalities and prescience of another day to come. Certainly not the magic hour when the sun set and dreams were created. Only now, in the daytime doldrums, the entertaining diversion of a five-foot-eleven redhead in stretch Lycra would be welcome at the Meadows. I gathered the ducks back into the bucket, grabbed my keys off the dressertop and headed to the well-heeled world of Memphis's most lush country club.

Chapter Thirteen

The lot was full at the club, the day's light breeze bringing out more than the usual number of players and enticing them to stay. I cruised up and down several rows of parked cars before finding an open spot between a red Mercedes convertible and a Lexus sport utility vehicle with doctor's plates. I parked, walked toward the clubhouse with its sweeping verandas, following two blondes with well-toned calves and honey tans, sporting pink and white gym bags and lightly swinging sheathed tennis rackets in the same rhythm as their hips. Always a huge fan of illusion, the club had been Paul's natural habitat. I grabbed the front door's shiny brass ring and went inside.

I was greeted by an artificial coolness, a cistern of extravagant flowers and several second looks. I smiled at no one in particular as I crossed the lobby, ignoring the signs declaring Members Only.

"Can I help you?" A smooth-faced brunette stood behind an oak desk. She wore a polo shirt and shorts and had the healthy color and fit body considered the quintessential look of the American woman.

"I'm Silver LeGrande, Penny." I read the name tag above her perky left breast.

Her smile and gaze turned vague.

"I was married to Paul Chumsky."

The almond-brown eyes narrowed at the corners. The involuntary tilt of her head suggested she had slept with Paul and was comparing herself to others that had come before.

Assessment complete, she said, "I'm sorry." She heard what she said. "I don't mean about you being married to Paul. I mean about…" She paused, searching for a delicate euphemism.

"Thank you," I said, feeling as genial and grand as old money. "Is Mason in?" Mason Hamm was the club manager.

"Let me buzz him."

"Thank you, Penny," I said, the surroundings forcing me to sound affected. As she called Mason's office, I stepped over to the wide curve of French windows looking out onto the acres of rolling, manicured lawns. I was still standing there, marveling at man's indulgence when I heard Mason's deep-voiced welcome. I turned into his embrace. He smelled of Ben Gay and barbecue.

I let him kiss my cheek and then, with a firm step backward, insisted he release me. He had a face neither handsome nor ugly and a penchant for plus-size women, he had once confided to me after too many mint juleps on an empty stomach.

I crinkled my nose. "Muscle soreness this morning, ribs for lunch?"

He laughed, putting his arm around my shoulders as we started down the hall. "C'mon, let's have a seat in the lounge, have a drink and share stories about Paul." He stopped to look at me. "I miss that bastard," he said with such simple sincerity I forgave him for pigeonholing my breast beneath his armpit.

"I miss him, too, Mason."

We walked past the formal and informal dining rooms, the ballroom that could seat four hundred, to the walnut-carved bar overlooking the Olympic-size pool.

"Have you eaten? We've got a crabcake that would make you stand up and cheer for the South."

I shook my head. "Just iced tea, please."

He nodded, signaled to the cocktail waitress and ordered two iced teas.

"How are you, Mason?"

He leaned back in his chair, patted the small pouch of his stomach. "Aging gracefully."

"Amen," I said.

"You've got a few good years before you fall apart, honey." Mason winked at me.

"Stop sweet-talking me, Mason." I patted his cheek. "Next you'll have me blushing like a peach in springtime."

"Be a sight to behold." He grinned, his wink slightly more good ol' boy then lecherous. Paul had once told me Mason had grown up above his family's gas station, living on white bread and lard and smelling of grease. For a moment I saw that little boy sneaking a peek at the girlie calendar in the garage, ogling Miss July curled around a V-12 twin-turbocharger as she beamed the smile of all women who had discovered the efficiency of mechanical devices.

I leaned forward. "You think Paul killed himself, Mason? Killed that stripper, then himself."

He grew thoughtful. His gaze dropped down to the floor. "I can't rightly say, Silver. You work with someone for years, think you know them…" His gaze came back to my face, moved in. "But how much do we really know anyone? If he did do it, I blame the liquor."

"Nothing else?" I probed. "Nobody else?"

"What are you getting at, Silver?" He put on the protective air of the manager of a championship golf course and exclusive country club whose members preferred to keep their scandals out of the public arena.

"Tell me about Fiona Herschmann."

He gave me an appraising look. "What do you already know?"

"I know she was sleeping with Paul."

"Do you mind if I'm blunt, Silver?"

"Actually I prefer it."

"I believe you're aware that the fact Fiona Herschmann was sleeping with Paul does not make her unique among the Meadows' female population."

"No, but I believe the fact her husband and her lover both died only a few days apart does."

"Coincidence."

I gave an Auntie snort.

He looked surprised. "You don't think so?"

"Two men intimately involved with the same woman die only a few days apart." I pulled out my trump card. "And in almost the same manner. Coincidence? No, I don't think so."

"Ben Herschmann died of a heart attack."

"He hung himself."

One brow quirked. "You're mistaken."

"Tell that to Ben."

"You're certain?"

I nodded.

Mason frowned at his tea. "Our members expect discretion."

I smiled my stripper's smile. "I am nothing if not discreet, Mason."

"Right," he drawled.

"If the situation warrants it."

He smiled. I could have a shot yet.

I crossed my legs, propped my elbow on my knee, my chin on my fist, leaned in as if to seal a deal. "Two men dead. Maybe murdered. There might be more. Obviously this is one of those situations that warrants prudence." God bless English Comp 101.

He smiled like an old friend, looked pointedly at my iced tea. "Prudence has a place in your life now, does it?"

"There was a time it didn't."

"Ahh, yes." Paul leaned back, folding his hands on his paunch, reflective. "It certainly wasn't Paul's forte."

"If it was, he'd probably be alive today." I smiled, showing remarkable patience. Patience and prudence. Soon I'd be dull as dirt. "So…?" I led him.

"Fiona Herschmann. The ladies don't like her."

"And she could give a flying fig, right?" I interrupted.

Paul paused to punish me. When he decided I was sufficiently chastised, he continued. "No, she does not give a flying fig."

"Was Paul her first affair?" I couldn't restrain myself. So much for prudence and patience. Sounded like a bad Vatican act, anyway.

"Hell, no. There had been others."

"The woman's not exactly a shrinking violet."

"No, but this is the first time she had taken a lover from the club."

"Discretion?" I ventured.

"Maybe." Mason shrugged. "Maybe she never found anyone here before appealing."

"She told me she fell in love with Paul."

· Mason looked surprised. "When did she tell you that?"

"At Paul's funeral."

Mason's surprise increased. "So much for discretion, huh?"

I looked around the richly appointed room, saw through the wide windows, the sun shimmering off the pool's surface. "Hate to burst your bubble, Mason, but Shangri-la, here, isn't exactly the real world."

"True." He looked at me dead-on. "Did you believe her?"

"I had no reason not to. I fell in love with Paul once, too." I shrugged. "Lightening strikes."

"Is that why you're so obsessed about his death?"

I leaned in again, only this time not smiling. "What I'm obsessed about, Mason, is the truth."

"Ahh, truth." Mason nodded as if wise.

"You don't know anything, do you?" I realized.

"Discretion, Silver."

I called him an indiscrete name.

He smiled. "For a minute there, I thought you'd gone soft on me. Be one of the world's great losses." He winked at me—friendly, not suggestive. "The word was Fiona had her playmates, her husband had his."

"One big, happy family."

"In a manner of speaking. The arrangement suited all parties involved."

"So why is one party dead? Along with the other party's lover?"

"If I had the answer to that, don't you think I would have told someone by now?"

"I don't know. Would you?"

"I'm not discreet when it comes to possible murder, Silver. Especially with that detective who has all the ladies licking their chops every time he comes into the club, breathing down my neck."

So Serras was doing his homework after all.

"All I really know was someone was in trouble. And whoever it was, they'd asked Paul for his help."

"What kind of trouble?"

"Paul didn't say."

"Discretion?" I questioned, one eyebrow arching.

"It was no small part of Paul's success here at the club."

"So you don't have details?"

Mason shook his head. "Only a sense it was serious. Big time."

I remembered what Billie said that afternoon at the club. *Paul did it for the money but he did it to help Della, too.*

"And it was someone here at the club," Mason revealed.

"A member?" Not Della?

Mason nodded.

All this time I'd had it wrong. Paul hadn't been working with Della. He'd been working against her.

"Did Paul say anything about being paid for his assistance?"

"What makes you ask that?"

"When Paul died, he had over half a million dollars spread out over several accounts. That's a lot of tips for a country club pro."

"He didn't say anything, but they must have been paying him."

"So it was someone with money. And a lot to lose."

"That describes ninety-five percent of our membership."

"Whoever it was, if they went to Paul, they must have had a reason." I thought out loud. "The dancer found murdered the day before Paul's death, the one whose G-string was around his neck, I think she was putting the screws to someone."

"Blackmail?" Mason caught on.

"I'd worked with the girl at Billie's. Whoever went to Paul must had known that, along with the fact he was once married to me."

We stared at each other.

"I know Paul was good on the greens and between the sheets, but putting himself in the middle of an extortion scheme?" Mason questioned. "With all due respect to the dead, whoever picked Paul had picked the wrong savior."

Only they didn't realize it, I thought, until after they killed him.

"So, if this stripper—"

"Della," I supplied.

"So if Della was blackmailing someone here at the club that explains why she was taken out of the picture," Mason noted.

"But that still leaves one more problem. One more person who knows what happened."

"Paul," Mason's eyes narrowed. "I'll bet that's the way the bastards planned it all along. Take out the source of trouble. Get rid of the other chumps involved. Everyone lives happily ever after."

I reviewed who was dead. Della, Paul, Ben, Lucy. They must have each known something. "Do you remember the first time Paul mentioned anything about someone being in trouble, asking for his services?"

"I'd say it was about six months ago."

Right around the time Paul had hooked up with Fiona. Adrienne had said the scuttlebutt around the club was Fiona had pursued Paul. Had she come to him for help? Had her husband been in trouble?

On the other hand, the morning of Paul's funeral, Fiona had said Paul had come on to her, that she had assumed her husband had asked him to keep an eye on her. Had her husband hired Paul to make sure Fiona behaved herself? Then why were Ben and Paul dead and Fiona showing up in scarlet at funerals?

"Was Paul sleeping with anyone else when he was seeing Fiona?"

"Paul wasn't the type to kiss and tell."

Damn discretion.

"How about before he started the affair with Fiona? Did he mention anyone?"

"I didn't keep a score card, Silver. And neither did he." His gaze turned sly and his voice low. "But cocktail hour is coming up. Feed a few green apple martinis to these ladies and before dinnertime, you'll have a list of who's who."

I smiled. "Did you tell the police everything you told me?"

"Pretty much."

"Detective Serras?"

Mason nodded.

I leaned back in my chair, sipped my tea. Through the wide windows that overlooked the pool, a large straw hat with pink gardenias caught my attention. Its wide brim flopped over the wearer's neck, across her face, revealing only a pair of hibiscus-red lips and hot-pink hoop earrings big as oranges. The body was covered in a vibrant caftan made even more colorful in contrast to the timid pastels and mundane solids surrounding her. Give her a set of maraccas and the dame was a one-woman Carnivale. I shook my head. I didn't have to take a second look. Auntie Peggilee.

Her faithful sidekick took up the slack behind her in a bathing suit no more than a set of strings knotted at strategic places that would have had Rocco hyperventilating and Herbie Bloomberg calling convents.

Obviously Auntie and Adrienne were unaware of the club's preference for discretion.

"What about a man named Doyle? Does that ring a bell?"

Mason squeezed his brow and thought. After a few seconds he shook his head. "No one that I know."

I straightened up in my chair, set my glass on the table. "I think Della had something these people wanted. I think Paul had it, too. Insurance purposes. Once he saw what happened to Della, he must have figured they were going to kill him, too. So he double-crossed them. Whatever it is everybody is looking for, they still want it. And they think I might have it."

Mason's expression turned grave. "Are you in trouble, Silver?"

"Not so far today." I smiled as I pushed my chair back. "But if you hear anything more, I'd appreciate it if you give me a call."

"Sure." He stood.

"Could you give me a minute before we go down to Paul's office." I looked toward the pool where Adrienne was slicking herself up with oil and Auntie was peering over the tops of her sunglasses, casing the joint. "I see some people I know at the pool, and I'd like to say hello."

"Sure. Have Penny at the front desk page me when you're ready."

I left the lounge, walked down the steps to the pool, stepping out into a thick heat that made me want to curse everything, but, most of all, Tennessee in July. I weaved between chaise lounges and exposed flesh to Auntie and Adrienne and their eagle eyes.

"Afternoon, ladies." I perched on the end of Auntie's chaise. "Thought you preferred it in the buff in the backyard?"

"Doesn't everyone?" Auntie noted. Her gaze never stopped moving.

"So why aren't you home bronzing your breasts like most women your age?"

Auntie's eagle gaze landed on me. "I could ask you the same question." She stretched back on the chaise. "I decided to see how the other half lives." She languidly raised her hand, signaling a tanned young man in khaki shorts and a white polo shirt with the Meadows crest over the pocket. He came toward us with a tray and a thin white towel draped over his belt.

Auntie gave him a toothy smile, her hat's wide brim lending her a mysterious air. "Chad," she purred, reading the waiter's name tag. "Do you have any of those fou-fou drinks with those little cute umbrellas in it?"

Chad smiled knowingly. "We've got a peach colada that comes in a coconut shell."

"Divine." Auntie batted her eyelashes at him. To his credit, Chad kept his expression sincere and his eyes on Auntie despite Adrienne with her strategic strings. The boy would either be a gigolo or a politician. I wondered if Fiona had found him yet.

"Only, no alcohol please. My one friend is too young. My other is too wise. And one sip of libation and you might have to scrape me off the deck." She smiled at the handsome Chad in a way that said she didn't find the idea without promise.

"Three peach colada mocktails coming right up, ladies," he promised and, with a smile, left to get our drinks. We all watched him go.

I sighed. "Long way from the Oyster."

"Yes, indeedie," Auntie agreed, her gaze scanning the surroundings before it returned to peer at me over the top of her sunglasses. "But don't let it fool you. Death doesn't discriminate, darlin'."

She had a point.

Auntie edged up on the chair seat until her hat's wide brim shaded me, too. She dropped her voice, her gaze flickering from side to side to make sure no one was listening. "Check it out," she told me. "Perfect vantage point."

I twisted around, saw the restaurant, lounge up above, a smaller bar and snack hut on the lower pool level. I turned back. Beyond Auntie were the rolling miles of greens and golf carts.

"From here, you can practically see everything going on in this joint."

"And what is it you're looking for?"

Her gaze rested on me once more. "Same thing as you." Her voice dropped an octave. "The killer."

"And you think you'll find whoever that is here?"

"Two people associated with the place are dead."

I almost said "coincidence" before I remembered who I was talking to. "Two people associated with the Oyster are dead, too."

Adrienne looked up from trying to smooth the stubble on her calves. "Can we go there, too?"

"Not in that suit," I told her.

She smiled wickedly. These two were starting to worry me. "You shouldn't even be here. You should be home saying no to Rocco or divining the square root of googolplex. Your father is already worried that I've put you in harm's way, and here you are, nearly naked and on the front lines."

"Here you go, ladies." The waiter swept down on us, handing us each a coconut shell filled with a creamy, pale-orange drink embellished with an umbrella and fruit, skewered on a small plastic sword.

Adrienne slipped Chad her membership card. "Put these on the Bloomberg account, please." She smiled prettily. "Add fifteen percent extra for yourself."

Chad smiled down at the glistening Adrienne. "Anything else, ladies?" he asked hopefully.

"These ought to keep us quite happy for now, Chad," Auntie told him. She took a long sip of the concoction, waggled her fingers goodbye.

"If you need anything else, let me know." Chad shot a smile that tempted even me.

"Oh, yes." Adrienne practically panted. She flopped back on the lounge chair, took a large gulp of colada and sighed happily. I had to admit death and danger seemed like too very remote possibilities at the Meadows.

I downed a third of my drink, set it on the poolside table. "Actually I came to clean out Paul's office, but since you two are hell-bent on hanging around here, you could make some chitchat with the other ladies, maybe learn if Paul was sleeping with anyone before Fiona came into the picture or maybe while Fiona was already in the picture?"

"You think the murders might have something to do with one of Paul's affairs?"

"It's a stab in the dark but his boss said Paul mentioned something about helping out someone in trouble. Someone here at the club."

"Who?" Auntie jumped right on it.

"Paul never said, but I think that's where the money in his accounts came from. Paul's boss said a few martinis and these ladies will tell you their real age. Maybe they can tell us something else."

I stood. "But be careful." I pointed a warning finger at them both. "And no Oyster. Understand?"

The look Auntie gave me in response said

that she'd do as she damn pleased. But her head tipped toward Adrienne and, with a small shake, told me poolside was as close as Adrienne would get to death and danger. As I walked away, I doubled my resolve to solve these cases before anyone else got hurt—including myself.

It was cool and dim inside the building. I stopped, blinking until my pupils focused. I climbed the stairs to the lobby, asked fresh-faced Penny to buzz Mason for me. He appeared a few minutes later and led me to a small, windowless room that had served as Paul's office.

"The police looked through the desk and file cabinets but didn't take anything back to the station."

"By police, you mean Serras?"

"Two uniforms came the first time. Serras came later that day. When I told him someone had been in that morning, he seemed surprised, said he wanted to take a look anyway in case the two other cops missed something."

"Did Serras find anything?"

"Left empty-handed as far as I know."

"What about Paul's locker? They take a look in there too?"

Mason nodded. "Dumped his golf bag,

turned his club blazer inside out, fingered the lining."

"Nothing?" I asked.

"Nothing. Let me grab you a couple of storage boxes to pack up anything you might want to keep."

After Mason left, I circled the small, airless room. I stopped in front of several fake wood shelves lining the wall behind Paul's desk. Trophies filled the shelves. I rubbed the dust film off one gold plate on a marble base. The Augusta Invitational, 1996. Paul had come in third in May. We'd married in October. Banner year for us both.

"Here you go."

I started at the sound of Mason's voice. He came over, looked at the tallest trophy. "He had his moments, huh?"

"More than most people."

Mason put his arm around my shoulders, gave me a squeeze. "Take your time, honey. When you finish, just call the front desk. I'll have Penny send some caddies down to carry the boxes up to your car."

"Thanks, Mason."

He started toward the door.

"What about his locker?" I remembered. "Will I be able to get into that?"

He stopped. "It's off the men's locker room in a special section reserved for employees. If you want to go now, I can unlock it for you before I go."

"Sure." I picked up a box, followed him out the door, down a short hall and took a sharp right, ending up before a door that said "Employees Only."

Mason opened the door. "Let me check and make sure no one's in here first." He stepped inside, returned a few seconds later. "All clear. Come on in."

I moved past him into the locker room that smelled of disinfectant and sweat socks.

"Here we are." Mason stopped before a locker, took a master key from his pocket and opened the lock. "Paul had had a combination lock but we sawed it off when the police came."

I remembered the small key on Paul's key ring I still carried in my purse, the one I had assumed opened his locker. The locker door swung open. Taped to its inside was a picture of me in a white strapless dress, an orchid pinned in my hair. My wedding day.

"He told me once he never stopped loving you, Silver."

"He was drunk," I said tenderly.

"Sure he was, but he meant it."

"Get the hell out of here, Mason."

"Yes, ma'am. I'll leave the door open so if anyone comes in, they'll know someone is in here."

He left me alone with the metal lockers and memories. I gingerly pulled the photo off the door. A golf cardigan hung on a hook. I pushed it aside, saw taped to the back wall of the locker several nudies. I smiled. So much for sentimentality.

There was a small, rectangular leather case on the locker's top shelf. I set the photo on the shelf and took down the case and unzipped it. Inside I found high-end men's toiletries. I fumbled through the items as if the answers I sought could be found in an upscale shaving kit. All I found were overpriced grooming items and an unused condom. I zippered the case back up, dropped it into the box along with the sweater and the photo. I carried the box back to Paul's office, sat down at his desk, disheartened. I pulled open the drawers. In a deep lower left-hand drawer, I found a half-empty bottle of Jim Beam. I took it out, set it on the desk in front of me, eyed it. I reached for my rubber band, pulled it back from my wrist. It broke.

Chapter Fourteen

I gripped the bottle's neck, my fingers tap dancing against the glass. I suspected if I opened the lower right-hand drawer, I'd probably find another bottle. Scotch or brandy. If I got up, went to the file cabinet, I might find another. My fingers relaxed, loosened their grasp around the bottle. There was a small mini-refrigerator in the corner. Paul liked beer, too. Especially after being out in the heat. He'd told me once the cans were a pain. He didn't want clients or management coming into the office, seeing the cans in his garbage pail at ten in the morning.

So what do you do with them? I'd asked.

Stick them in a small garbage bag, tie it up and hide them in the drop ceiling over the desk.

My eyes rolled upward. The wide, rectangular panels fit into a thin-framed grid work suspended below the floor above, creating a space of several feet easily accessible by pushing up on the panel and moving it to the side. Slide the panel back into the grid work's grooves and no one would know the difference. The ceilings were especially practical for hiding pipes, duct-work and all kinds of secrets.

I set the bottle aside, stood and climbed up on the desk. Crouching, I slid over the panel directly above my head, straightened, poking my head into the space between the ceiling and floor above. A garbage bag of beer cans was at my ear. I pushed them aside, saw another farther back. I turned to the other side, peered into the gloom. A small box shape, a glint of silver. I reached out, straining on my tiptoes. My fingertips brushed cool metal, but the object was too far away to get a grip on it.

I climbed down off the desk, grabbed a putter from Paul's golf bag leaning in the corner, climbed back up on the desk and, using the club, hooked it around the metal box and pulled it toward me. A soon as it was close enough, I grabbed it. In my hands was a small metal cash-box with a lock. Pressing it to my chest, I climbed down off the desk.

The box was small but heavy, made of steel. I found Paul's key ring in my purse, separated the one small key, slipped it into the lock.

I turned the key to the right, heard a click. I

lifted the top slowly. Inside was a pile of photographs. Full color. Digital detail. There was a frontal shot of a large man in heels and a garter on a stool, a leather thong around his neck.

The last laugh.

A woman was kneeling before the man, her back to the camera. She had long, red hair.

It wasn't me.

I'm not one to judge, but this kind of scene would never do it for me. Nor would any guy who thought high heels were a path to pleasure. Try dancing three sets a night in them.

I remembered the long, red wig in the lockers at the Oyster. I leaned in to examine the picture closer, but the woman's face was hidden. I held the picture up to the light, squinted, saw the delicate rose vine high on the buttock, one D. The rest was covered by the long red hair. My stomach bottomed out.

I set the picture down. I heard Billie's voice.

You don't know what you're getting into, chère. Della and Paul are dead, Silver. You pursue this and you'll die, too.

Had Billie known about the pictures? If so, why hadn't she told the police? Or had she? But they had been persuaded not to go public with the information.

…it was someone with money. And a lot to lose.

I looked at the man in his mother's worst nightmare. He was gray, midfifties, overweight with skinny legs even the heels didn't help. I didn't know him. I stared at the strange tableau for several minutes. I thought of Rocco's explanation on how Vito Figuero had stayed on top for so long. "He gives them what they need. Then, when the time is right, they give him what he needs."

Had that been Della's strategy? Had she dangled a garter belt and debauchery, then had someone click the cameras, guaranteeing her needs would be met? What had she wanted? Not money. Della had died as broke as she had been born. I thought of Della's brother's death. Justice? Revenge? Had that been Della's desire?

The next picture was a close-up, the man's face contorted in exquisite agony. Quite a candid. I shuddered.

I turned the shots slowly facedown into a neat pile as I looked at each one. Beneath the photos in the metal box was a video. The cassette's colorful cover was the Walt Disney film *Dumbo*. Paul and his last laughs. I found a manila folder for the photos, dropped them and the video into my purse. I slipped out of the office, through the employees' locker room and out the back exit, made a wide circle to the parking lot, trying to blend.

I was almost to my car when I heard my name. I swung toward the sound as if ready to strike, only to face the feckless Fiona. She stepped back, a bemused smile on her face.

"All that delicious energy. Cat on a hot tin roof, darlin'."

I saw dark moons under her eyes, wondered if her prescriptions had run out.

"What brings you to the sanctified Meadows?"

"Sentimentality."

She smiled. "Does the best of us in, darlin.'" She looked around. "I'm here because the martinis are always dry and the ass kissing is an art. Her eyes turned sad for a moment, the circles beneath them darker. "Are you leaving?"

I nodded. Although the idea of a girl talk with Fiona, whose stories I'm certain could rival mine, was enticing, I was anxious to get the photos and tape to Serras. "Don't say let's do lunch sometime or I'll have to slap you."

She released a lovely laugh. "Sometimes someone should." She said. Her voice withered. "Sometimes someone should."

I contemplated her, remembering her conversation with the mysterious man outside of Billie's the night of Paul's funeral. Sometimes someone had. "What did your husband look like, Fiona?"

She gave me the same deep search. She withdrew a Gucci wallet from her Prada bag, flipped it open and held out to me a picture of her smiling at the camera beside a broad, imposing gray-haired man. This time he was wearing black tie, not women's lingerie.

I looked up into her eyes, wondered if she knew.

She averted her gaze, looked to the greens. "He could be quite charming when the moment presented itself." She looked at me as if expecting agreement. I said nothing. First rule of interrogation.

"Most of the time, though, he was a total bastard. Do you have time for a drink?" she offered without missing a beat.

"I don't drink."

She nodded as if it was the answer she expected. "Neither did I once upon a time."

"What happened, Fiona?"

She stared at me as if trying to decide whose side I was on.

"I know about the pictures."

She looked away. I feared I'd lost her.

"The pictures," she murmured. My heart jump-started.

"I guess they began coming about six months ago." I took a stab, held my breath."

She delicately tilted her head and eyeballed me. "So Paul did tell you."

I said nothing.

She closed her eyes, inhaled deeply. When she opened them, I saw almost relief. I still hadn't released my breath.

"I didn't know about them at first. Ben asked Paul to look into it." She smiled and looked pretty instead of bone tired. "I was first on the prime-suspect list."

"Why?"

She shrugged. "Once you have something, it's hard to give it up."

"And you were about to lose something you had?"

"I was Ben's second wife. I broke up his first marriage. Ben and I, we deserved each other really." Her mouth twisted in a rueful smile. "But relationships like ours, they don't last. I'd signed a prenup that I violated before we celebrated our second anniversary." Her mouth angled tighter, and again she looked older than her years. "I have a self-destructive streak that will see me all the way to hell."

Her husband wasn't exactly a choirboy.

"It very well could have been me with the

Kodak camera, but it wasn't. Someone else beat me to it."

"Della Devine?"

"That's what Paul was hired to find out."

That explained the money, the easy lifestyle. "Why Paul?"

"Ben had a thing for strippers."

"The girl in the photo?"

She nodded. "Ben knew Paul had once been married to you, that he still had a lot of contacts among the clubs."

"Why was Della blackmailing your husband?"

"Ben had one of the largest trucking companies in the southeast. He had several major contracts with the federal government. Supply shipments, things of that nature."

"The military?"

"Fort Grant was one of his largest customers. Your friend was working for the competition."

"Vito Figuero?"

"Vito and his boys wanted Ben to come work for them, but first they wanted information to take down a certain supply operation coming out of Fort Grant. I guess it was cutting into their business somehow. Poor Ben was in quite a pickle. If he left his current partners, they would probably kill him. If he didn't, then Vito would be sure photos of him in thigh-highs and heels would be as popular as party favors. Quite a pickle." Fiona barked a sharp laugh.

"So your husband decided to go to work for Vito?"

"He set up a preliminary meeting. Afterward Della provided the entertainment. Another form of friendly persuasion, I suppose."

Her gaze seemed to lose focus. Stay with me, Fiona, I prayed.

"Paul captured the whole party in Technicolor."

I thought of the video in my purse, went cold. "He was there?"

"No. He and Della, they didn't really care what Vito and Ben did or didn't do. I think she got scared and told Paul about the meeting, the time and place. He had set up a recorder on automatic timer. He didn't know…I didn't know…"

"Why did he set up a recorder?"

Fiona brushed back a bang. I saw her hand was trembling. "For me."

"Your portfolio?" I ventured.

"Opportunity presents itself, a girl's got to take it." Fiona spoke matter-of-factly. Yet her hands shook. "If the people Ben worked for didn't kill him after he went over to Figuero's, once Figuero's people got what they wanted, they would have. They would have killed me, too." She shrugged. "They still might." Her gaze zeroed in on me. "A lady needs leverage." She shifted her gaze. Her voice was not as strong. "I didn't know they were going to do that to the girl."

"And the tape was still rolling?"

Fiona's composure slipped another notch. "Imagine," she murmured.

"Did you see it? Did you see who killed Della?"

She shook her head. "When Paul learned about Della's death, he said no more. End of deal. He was going to turn the tape over to the police. We fought. I was angry, I told him he and the tape would end up in the river."

"Is that why he didn't turn the tape over?"

"I don't know. I don't think he knew what to do. There was a lot of discussion on the tape between Ben and Figuero's people. Names, dates. People who could become very unpleasant. He hid the tape while he was trying to figure out a way to do the right thing and stay alive in the process."

Maybe that explained Paul's call to Johnny Flint. Maybe if something happened to him, he wanted someone without a stake in the scheme, an outsider, to know about the tape.

"A lawyer came down from Kingsley's office the night Paul was picked. Why didn't he talk to him?"

"He did. He told him about the tape, the names, the dates. Michael Kingsley works for the same people Ben did. Important people. Kingsley's job is to protect those people. People named on that tape. Paul was negotiating for protection. But someone got to him before…" Her hands made a small, helpless gesture.

"Figuero's people?"

"He was working both sides of the fence, plus he knew too much. Just like Della. He didn't even get a chance to threaten them with the tape before one of their whores slipped him that date-rape drug, then they dolled him up, hoisted him high. They could at least have let the man die with a little dignity. I'll bet the bastards had a chuckle all the way home."

"But the M.E.'s report only showed high alcohol levels in Paul's blood."

"The drug doesn't show in the blood. Only in the urine. That is, if you test for it."

"Sounds like you've been talking to Figuero's camp."

Her expression became bland, but her eyes were clear. "Negotiation. A very fine art. Complicated, really. And the only reason I'm still alive at the moment."

I thought of the conversation I'd overheard the night at Billie's after Paul's funeral.

"If anything happens to you, the tape surfaces." I picked up the ball. "Something neither party prefers."

"Quite a pickle."

"Only one problem. I thought Paul didn't tell you where the tape was?"

Fiona smiled, catlike. "He didn't."

I smiled back. You gotta love this lady.

"Not that I didn't look like hell. No one has found the tape."

Until ten minutes ago.

"But they bought your story."

Let's just say no one is ready to prove me a liar yet."

"I heard you the night of Paul's funeral outside Billie's. You were talking to someone, a man."

"Kingsley." Fiona spit the name.

"It was Kingsley who set the goon on me?" Fiona nodded.

"You could have gone to the police, told them about the tape."

She released a lovely rich laugh that told me I was a fool "Only one problem," she mocked me. "I had no tape. "The police had already made up their mind about the case, anyway."

"How did your husband die, Fiona?"

I took her by surprise. Her face lost its ease. "He had a heart attack."

I waited.

Steel seeped back into her features. "In the middle of an autoerotic orgasm. But if his heart hadn't exploded, the strap around his neck would have strangled him. Ben was well aware how easily something could go wrong in this particular scenario. I imagine it was part of the intrigue. He was careful with his equipment, his precautions. Except this time."

"Do you think your husband was trying to kill himself?"

"I think we're all trying to kill ourselves, one way or another."

"Was your husband alone when this happened?"

She looked at me hard. "No."

"Who was with him?"

"Me."

She leaned in. True confession time. "Man's fatal flaw," she said, deep-throated. "Desire."

She didn't wait for any of it to set in. She was already moving toward the club. I went after her.

"Fiona?"

She stopped.

"Did you pull the chair out from under Paul?"

"Yeah, from the moment he met me," she said without turning to look at me. She stood a moment longer, her back to me. "Figuero's people shouldn't have killed Paul," she said with a rare regret. "Not that way. He deserved that much."

She really had loved him.

Fiona straightened. "It's a shame you don't drink," she said, any trace of anguish gone from her voice. She turned and started again toward the club with determined steps. "The martinis here really are divine."

I watched her elegant, long-legged stride until she disappeared inside the clubhouse. I got in my car, headed downtown to Serras.

He was in his office on the third floor, filling in paperwork. The building was old, poorly insulated and it soaked up the heat like a sponge. Portable fans created an artificial breeze and an undercurrent of white noise. I stepped into his office without invitation, pulled the video and manila folder out of my purse and plopped them on top of the form he had been scribbling on. He looked at the Walt Disney graphics on the videocassette, slowly slid his gaze up to me.

"Already saw it."

I pushed over some papers to make a small space to perch myself on the edge of his desk. I crossed my legs high on the thigh and leaned over him. "Not this version."

"Did you bring popcorn, too?"

"Watching this, you won't have much appetite."

"You underestimate me, LeGrande."

I looked down into those dark eyes, remembered the moment he'd entered me. "That's one mistake I never made."

He opened the manila folder, looked at the photos, back up at me. "Are these the outtakes?"

"Previews." I slinked off the desk, straightened up. "Find us the closest television with a VCR player, Serras." I fluttered my hands like a Bob Fosse chorus girl. "It's show time."

As we walked out of his office, he put his hand on the small of my back in that proprietary manner that had made me cause some men great pain. Serras was safe. I, however, was not. I stepped away from his touch.

He led me to a small conference room with a television set on the top shelf of a metal cart, a VCR player on the shelf beneath it. He took out the cassette, shoved it into the player. As he was about to press Play, my pants began to vibrate. I pulled out my cell phone, frowned at the number on the screen.

"Hello."

Serras waited as I took the call.

"Silver, it's Mason. There was an accident at the club. Your aunt and her friend, the girl, her father is a member here." He was talking in spurts, scaring me totally.

"They were in the sauna. Something happened. The door wouldn't open. The temperature regulator malfunctioned. When we finally got them out of there, it was 180 Fahrenheit."

I made a small, hoarse, desperate sound that caused Serras to take a step toward me. I raised my palm, halting him.

"Your aunt had a piece of pipe that she and the other girl banged on the door with to get someone's attention. They're on their way to Memphis General now to be treated for hyperthermia. The EMTs started pumping them with potassium and electrolytes as soon as they arrived."

"They're going to be okay?" I prayed.

"The medics said we got to them in time. I'm so sorry, Silver. I have no idea how this happened. We've never had an accident like this—"

"It was no accident, Mason."

I disconnected, faced Serras. "I gotta go."

"What happened?"

"Auntie Peggilee, Adrienne." I saw my hands lift as if looking for something to hang on to. "Someone locked them in the sauna at the Meadows Country Club, jacked up the heat. I gotta go."

He ejected the tape, slipped it back into its case. "I'll drive you."

"I'm a big girl, Serras."

He was still walking beside me. "I've got a big siren."

"This is no time to talk dirty to me, Serras." My voice cracked. I was afraid my composure was next.

"Let me lock these up." He slipped into his office to get rid of the video and the folder and caught up with me in the hall. We were moving toward the stairs when two men stepped out of the stairwell.

"Serras," the one in uniform acknowledged. He looked familiar. The other man wore street clothes. He was big, wide, and when he turned, he looked directly at me and smiled as if we shared a secret. My instincts quivered like a tuning fork. Serras gave both men a nod as they headed into an office. The man in street clothes glanced over his shoulder once more before going into the room. He was still smiling.

I waited until we were on the next floor. "Who was that man in street clothes?"

"Leo Flesch. Worked Vice for years. Retired last year. Works part-time as a security consultant. Stops in now and then to check up on things, see the guys."

We reached the first floor, stepped out into a heat only slightly worse than inside the building.

"Friends of yours?" I asked Serras with a sidelong look.

"Worked with him when I was assigned Vice." He opened the car door for me. "Why?"

I remembered Billie's story about when Serras worked Vice. According to Billie, he was a clean cop. She had better be right. I slid in, looked at him from inside the car. "He seemed familiar."

Serras hesitated before he stepped away and closed the door. He wasn't buying it.

He showed his detective's shield to the nurse in the emergency room and got us immediate attention. We were shuttled into a room where Auntie and Adrienne lay on gurneys with tubes in their arms. Auntie's eyes were closed, her color gone. My breath hitched. Serras heard it before I left him at the doorway.

I took Adrienne's hand, bent over and kissed her. "What the hell—"

She smiled up at me, her face smooth and innocent. "It was the damnedest thing. I'm okay, really. But Auntie," she glanced at her roommate. "Being older…"

"I'm not dead yet," Auntie interrupted. She opened her eyes, smiled weakly at us both. I moved to her side.

"What's the problem, sugarpuss? I lost ten pounds, and Adrienne met the hottest medic this side of the Mason-Dixon line." She winked at me. "Not bad work for an afternoon." She looked past me, waggled a wave at Serras. "Hello, handsome. Did you come to interrogate me?" she asked hopefully.

"I have a few questions I'd like to ask you when you're ready."

"I was born ready, sweet pea." She patted the bed. "Bring your big, beautiful self right over here to Auntie Peggilee."

I looked down at the lady I loved on the white stretcher, her beehive held intact. The fear that had propelled me to this point was morphing into a white-hot rage. There are many ways to lose control. This was only one more. Auntie was entertaining Serras with her sauna saga as I slipped out of the room. A nurse walking toward me saw me flip open my cell phone.

"No cell phones in the hospital," she barked. "Their signals cause the monitors, electronic devices to go haywire." She stabbed a finger toward the door. "Outside."

I made my way to the parking lot, punched in a number.

"Yeah?" The mean male voice answered.

"You're dead, Doyle."

I heard a chuckle that caught at my insides. "How is Auntie? And your young friend? Haven't they heard safety standards for saunas warn a person not to exceed thirty minutes."

"I have what you want."

"Please, Silver, this is getting tiresome. Today was a warning. Next time your friends might not be so lucky. Keep sticking your nose where it doesn't belong, and it's going to get cut off. Along with sundry other body parts. I've only let you live this long because you amuse me."

"I have the pictures of Ben Herschmann."

"Ben Herschmann is dead."

"I have the video."

Complete silence.

"And I just met a friend of yours." I went for broke. "Leo Flesch."

The silence lasted a satisfying speechless second more.

"The only question now is whose side are you on. Kingsley's or Figuero's. Kind of a moot point at this moment. But by bet is Figuero, because Kingsley would have known about our previous chats. And he hasn't a clue. He's still keeping his fingers crossed that Fiona Herschmann is the only wild card he's got to deal with."

"What do you want?" Doyle was definitely not in a good mood. I, however, was.

"What Della wanted. What I won't get from you. Justice."

"How noble." Doyle had recovered. "Tell me, who will you get it from, Silver?" The voice was amused, deliberately provoking. It was a stripper's voice.

"Serras has the tape now."

I listened to the long laugh on the other end.

"Silver, Silver." Doyle's rhythmic reply told me he was shaking his head. "Who do you think was assigned to watch you?"

Chapter Fifteen

In the heat, I went cold. The rage inside me was white ice. Even as the anger overwhelmed, I clung to the thin lifeline of cool logic that was the only thing that could save me.

"Who do you think knew that all along?"

The laugh was warm but evil. "The game's over, sweet Silver. You played right into my hands. I'm going to miss you, but now that we've got what we want, we won't need your services any longer."

"Do you think I was stupid enough to turn over the video without making a copy?"

"You're bluffing." I heard a hesitation in the voice. The seed of doubt had been planted.

"Maybe I'm working for someone else, someone bigger than the Memphis boys in blue. Maybe you all played right into my hands." I was on a roll. Rage reined in by logic was a wonderful tool. I almost wished what I said was true. That would have been the cherry on top.

Laughter on the other end. "Silver, I am going to miss you."

"Don't get your hanky out yet, Doyle." I snapped closed my cell phone, marched inside, numb, remote, as if standing back, watching another woman having been made a fool of.

Serras was standing by Auntie's bedside, smiling at something she said. I looked at that gorgeous profile and understood the impulse that drove some people to murder. The possibility that Doyle could be playing with me as much as I had with him arose but was dismissed. Even if Doyle had been making it up, I couldn't take any chances. I trusted no one.

A doctor followed me into the room, checked Auntie, then Adrienne's vitals, proclaimed they wouldn't need to be admitted but he'd like to keep them here a few hours longer for observation. After the IVs were finished, as long as everything else was normal, he'd release them. As he was leaving, Herb hurried in.

"Lord, call the Mummers and we'll have a parade," Auntie said.

The doctor repeated his prognosis to Adrienne's father, assuring him his daughter was fine. Herb went to her, touched her brow.

"I'm fine, Daddy."

"She met an EMT who's premed," Auntie chimed in.

"So it wasn't a complete loss," Herb said, trying to smile. Fresh worry lines etched into his face. He looked at me but was gracious enough not to say it. Still it could have been tattooed across his forehead. *I told you so.*

It's almost over, Herb, I thought. Aloud, I asked, "You'll be here for a while?"

He nodded. I looked at Serras, my face masked. "If you're finished here, I'd like to go back to the station to pick up my car and come back."

He flipped closed his notebook. "I'm finished."

I went to Auntie to give her another kiss before I left.

"You heard the doctor, Silver. We're fine. There's no reason for you to hang around here for hours. Once they give us the okay, I'll call you on your cell phone, and you can pick me up."

"Auntie, I'm not so much worried about your current condition. I'm worried about what you might do next if I let you out of my sight." I leaned over, kissed her rice-paper-thin skin. "That goes for you, too, missy," I directed at Adrienne as I straightened.

Auntie and she released a snort in unison, shorthand for telling me to go to hell.

I turned to Serras, my expression sobering.

"Ready?" he asked.

I heard Auntie's voice in my head. *Born ready.* But I said nothing as I moved past him.

My seething silence on the ride back to the station warred with my primal instinct to cut Serras down to size. I opted for the safer choice of silence and hoped it would be attributed to worry about Auntie and Adrienne.

"What's on the video, Silver?" Serras broke the silence.

"Della's death."

He didn't even blink. The man was a classic. I suddenly wanted him to be clean, too. I could taste it in the slow grind of my molars. Turn off the oven. I was cooked.

"Also some stimulating conversation between Ben Herschmann and Vito Figuero's people."

He slanted his gaze to me. "You found the tape."

"I told you I was good, Serras."

"You showed me, too," he said before his half-lidded gaze left mine.

Another homicidal urge swept over me. "What happens now?"

"We watch the tape."

"And?" I looked for a clue on his handsome face.

"I'll take it to the county prosecutor's office."

"And they'll issue a warrant?"

He glanced at me, coplike, same hawk vision I'd adopted. "First we'll watch the movie."

I sank back into the seat and said nothing else until we got to the station. The video was locked, along with the pictures, in his desk drawer on the third floor of the city precinct. There was no way I could get it back now. If, as Doyle said, Serras was dirty, too, my presence would no longer be required in this cat-and-mouse game. Like Della, like Paul, I was now expendable. My only chance was to let someone else know that Serras had the video and the pictures should something happen to me.

I got out, slammed the door, headed toward my car.

"Hey." Serras's yell stopped me. He came toward me. "Where you going?"

"Back to the hospital. You've got what you need. There's nothing else I can do. You have to take it from here."

He studied me as if uncertain if he should let me go. "You're going to miss the big show."

I had the feeling I had already seen it. "You forget. I saw the coming attractions."

I drove hard and fast to Billie's. My first thought was to go to Fiona when I realized I'd just handed over the only thing keeping her alive. They'd kill us both, two for one. Efficiency had its place in professional murder.

Billie was in her office, going over the books when I rapped on her door. She didn't look surprised. Only a matter of time before my Silver returns to me, she probably told the others. I thought about the mess my life had become and wondered if her clairvoyance was correct.

"Which ones are those?" I nodded toward the account book opened before her. She closed it.

"You have your CPA license yet?"

"No."

"Then don't ask, *chère*." She smiled. She motioned toward a chair. I stayed standing.

"You knew about the pictures. Right from the beginning."

The smile dissolved from her face. "About six months ago your ex-husband came to see me. Said a friend of his was in a bit of a spot. Said he'd received an unmarked package in the mail. Inside were photos from a 'private party.' The woman in the photographs had long, red hair."

"Paul thought it was me."

She shook her head, the tight, slick curls on her crown catching the light. "He said no, never."

My ex-husband, a knight in shining armor, after all. I looked heavenward, mentally blew him a kiss.

"Still it looked like you. He was afraid someone else might make a mistake. He came here, hoping I might know something about this."

"Did you?"

She reached for a praline cream, slid the inlaid bowl toward me. I ignored it.

She unwrapped the candy, slipped it between her red lips. "How do you know about the pictures?"

"I found them."

Her expression became impressed. Her cheeks sucked in as she savored the sweet. "Where?"

"Paul's office at the Meadows."

She reached for another candy. "No one thought to look there until now?"

"They weren't in the usual hiding places."

"Obviously not," she said, casting approval. "Live with a man, you get to know his secrets."

"Mmm," she agreed, sliding the sweet between her lips.

"Did you see the photos?"

Billie shook her gracefully shaped head.

"It was Della in the photos."

Billie's heavily colored eyes shadowed. "I learned that later."

"From Paul?"

Billie nodded. She steepled her fingers, her long nails tapping rhythmically against each other. "I advised them both it would all come to no good."

"She went to Figuero's people."

"I suspected that after her tox screens came back clean. Figuero's people don't do business with coked-up chippies. Drugged up, you lose judgment, make bad choices. The junkie act must have been a cover, a diversion. Della must have known exactly what she was doing."

"Except she made one mistake. She trusted someone."

"Paul told me he tried to talk her out of it. After that, he tried to protect her." Billie laid her palms on the desk, spread her fingers like a fan and stared at her jeweled nails before she looked up at me. "She trusted Paul, Silver."

"She trusted Figuero's people more."

"The Fort Grant operation has been a thorn in Figuero's side since it came in, but even he couldn't do anything about it. Drug running sanctioned by the Federal government. Sweetest setup in the South. I remember after her brother's death, whenever the men came in from the base, Della was their best friend. She must have found out what she could and then she went to Vito's men."

"Why didn't she go to the FBI?"

"The bad guys were the Federal government. They'd killed her brother. They'd kill her, too."

"Only somebody got to her first." I said tightly. "The man who had hired Paul, Ben Herschmann, had decided he had no choice. He met with Figuero's people, was ready to give them information, which they would get into the right hands. Della was the party favor that night. She had done her job. She knew too much. Same with Paul."

"So Della and Paul were taken out because they knew too much."

"Somebody must have thought Lucy Champlain knew too much, too. No loose ends. Everything tied up neat and tidy. Until Ben Herschmann was found swinging from his closet door."

"Comedy of errors from what I hear." Billie skimmed the air with her long, sharp nails. "Ahh, life."

"Everything going according to plan until

that little snafu." I sank down into the chair, plopped my purse on my lap, sagged back against the upholstery and laughed. Hysterically. Billie watched me keenly.

I ended my laughter with a short sob. "I only have one more question," I said, wiping my eyes.

Billie interlaced her fingers and rested them on her belly and smiled at me like a Bourbon Street Buddha.

"Why didn't you go to the police about this?"

"She did," Doyle's voice said behind me.

I spun around, saw Leo Flesch. Next to him, with an automatic aimed between my plucked eyebrows, was the uniform I'd seen at the precinct, and I realized why he's seemed familiar. He was the detective that had questioned Paul the night of Della's death. The one Paul had taunted about the long, red scratches. "A hellcat," Paul had said. I remembered the cat at the Oyster Club, made the connection. Too little, too late. No wonder Paul had decided not to turn the tape over to the police. I looked at the men that had murdered Della, Paul, probably Lucy.

My head spun to stare at Billie. *Trust no one.* I was going to have it tattooed on my backside if I lived through this one. *Trust no one. And carry a .32.* I felt the pleasant weight of my purse on my lap. I turned back to the men.

"Doyle." I showed my teeth. "Finally I get to put an ugly mug with the voice."

Flesch smiled genially, the pale light in his eyes chilling and cold. "And you, sweet Silver, are never a disappointment. Actually Doyle is my middle name. My friends call me Leo."

"I'll call you rat bastard."

He let loose a harsh laugh. "I told you she'd be fun and games," he said to his sidekick. The policeman licked his lips, gave a sickly smile.

My pants began to vibrate. My fingers splayed on the chair cushions, gripping like a cat on a wall, twitched but didn't move.

"That's enough, gentlemen," Billie decided with obvious distaste. With a dignity even now I couldn't help but envy, she pushed away from her ornate desk, lifted her large body. "Take your business elsewhere."

"You heard the lady. Stand up, sweetheart," Flesch growled. The other man beside him gestured with the gun.

I stood, my expression full of loathing but my legs going loosey-goosey. As I got up, my hand brushed my trembling cellphone, pressed against it. It stopped quivering. I prayed I pressed Talk.

I gripped my purse and looked at Billie. "You knew everything all along. These are Figuero's meatheads, but Michael Kingsley was here the night of Paul's funeral. What are you? Switzerland?"

"As you can see, *chère,* it's not as simple as it seems."

I leaned over and spat in her face.

"Hey." The man with the gun stepped toward me but Billie held up her hand, stopping him. She plucked a tissue from the box on her desk, delicately wiped away the moisture.

"I told you, *chère.* I will not dance at your funeral." She dismissed us with a sweeping wave.

The gunman grabbed my arm and twisted it behind my back, shoving the gun into my spine. "Move, bitch."

"There's no reason to be rude, asshole," I told him above my heart slamming against my rib cage. Flesch chuckled, enjoying himself immensely.

We headed out into the hall to the back entrance. "So who made their screen debut? You?" I taunted Flesch. "I know your boy here had clean-up duty." I threw the cop behind me a teeth-baring smile. "Here kitty, kitty."

The gun jammed into my vertebrae as my

arm was wrenched out of its socket. I chose a swear word over a shriek of pain.

We reached the back door. "Where's Serras? Shouldn't he be at the party?"

"According to our reports, Serras already had his party." Flesch flashed me a smarmy smile. I would kill him for that alone. I tightened my white-knuckle grip on my purse as we stepped out into the back lot where the employees parked.

"Miss Silver." Coming right toward us was Sweet Sam. "How you doing today?" Sam glanced at the two men, puzzled.

"Fine and dandy, Sweet Sam." The last syllable came out a squeak. I forced a smile, tried to warn Sam with my eyes.

"Mind your own business now, boy," Flesch said. We moved past Sam, leaving him standing in the same spot with a confused expression. We were heading toward a van when I heard a mournful wail bearing down on us.

"No-o-o-o," Sam screamed, lunging at the man pushing the gun into my back. "No more trouble."

Both the cop and I went down. I jerked free as Sam and the cop wrestled on the ground. I scurried on my hands and knees to where my purse had flown out of my hand, its contents flung around the concrete when something hard and slim pressed against my temple.

"Looking for this?" Flesch asked. From the corner of my eye, I saw the mother-of-pearl handle. So much for the best-laid plans. Flesch yanked me up on my feet when I heard the shot behind us. We whirled.

"No-o-o-o-o!" I was screaming now as I saw Sam stretched out on the pavement, the blood blossoming across his gut.

"Get in the van." Flesch shoved me in the front seat, jumped into the driver's seat. He started the engine, threw it into reverse, slamming me into the seat. Tires squealing, he made a wide curve. As we flew through the parking lot, I heard the faint peal of sirens. I looked back and saw Billie kneeling beside Sam, her forehead pressed to his shoulder as sobs racked her body. The cop that had shot Sam had disappeared.

I called my captor every profanity I'd ever heard plus some new ones I made up along the way.

"Shut up," Flesch snarled, his amiable mood over.

"What are you going to do?" I snapped. "Kill me? Like you did Della? Paul? Lucy? Don't police pensions provide like they used to? Or do you just like it?"

We were heading to the river, a fact I indicated to whoever had called my cell phone by reading out loud the street signs and highway markers, familiar enough with the city from driving limousines that my mind did not reverse the route numbers.

We parked in front of a dilapidated wooden boathouse near the water, another fact I pointed out, hoping someone was listening. Flesch jumped out, dragging me with him. Prodding me with my own gun, he pushed me toward the structure half in ruins. We stepped into dim, close quarters, the floorboards creaking beneath our feet as if about to give way any minute. Flesch shoved me ahead of him into the center of the room, raised the gun.

"Shooting someone with their own gun." I edged back to the wall. "That's cold." *Irony* would be the Comp 101 term.

Flesch's lips pulled back into a wolfish sneer. "Maybe Memphis's finest can write this one off as a suicide, too. Not quite as colorful as your ex-husband's, though."

He released the safety. I broke into a deep sweat. Even Auntie's shoulder-length earrings weren't going to save me now. I took another step back, smiled. I reached for the halter ties around my neck.

Flesch motioned with the gun. "What are you doing?"

I played with the strings. I made my voice velvet. "Did you ever see me dance?" I stretched one halter string up high, untying it. I pulled both ties up, waving them behind my head as my body started to sway, my hips undulating in the same seductive rhythm as the water lapping on the shore. Flesch began to salivate. I smiled.

"You must have seen me?" I said in a kitten purr as I drew the ties in front of me. I let them dangle across my breasts, drawing the top of my halter down an inch, exposing a creamy swell of flesh while my fingers played across my stomach, drew small circles along the capris's waistband, fingered the zipper pull. "I put on quite a show."

I slowly smoothed my hands back up over the plane of my stomach, the curve of my breasts, reached behind my head and undid the barrette holding my hair. "I can put on a private show for you." I shook my hair free. It tumbled down my shoulders. I continued to sway, letting my hands play across my body, drawing him in. Mesmerized, Flesch took a small step toward me, then another. There was a loud crack. The floor gave way. Flesch's leg crashed through a rotten board. The gun fired. I was screaming as Serras burst into the room.

"Christ, it's about time you got here."

"Oh, hell, Serras. For a moment there, you scared me. Crashing in here like the damn cavalry." Flesch jerked his leg out of the rotten board, limped to a more secure spot, testing the boards gingerly. "You're just in time for the show."

I looked at Serras, a new sweat starting over the one already drying on my flesh.

"Show's over, Leo." He pointed his Glock at the other man.

Flesch smiled. "What do you mean, buddy?" I saw Flesch tighten his hand on my gun. He could shoot Serras, then me, say I did it and get away with it. Same M.O. as Mad Dog Barnes all those years ago.

Serras kept his gun tight on Flesch. "You forget, Leo. I'm the clean cop."

"What are you telling me? You were undercover?" The goofy grin on Flesch's face looked a little uncertain. His arm twitched.

"The department knew Figuero had people inside. Now they have proof." Serras's voice went low and ugly. "I saw what you did to that woman."

"C'mon, Serras. She was a piece of garbage.

You and I worked together. I'm a cop. You wouldn't shoot another police officer."

"That's another thing you forgot, Leo. I'm famous for it."

Flesch went for his gun but Serras already had the advantage. The blast caught Flesch point-blank between the eyes. He flew backward several feet, slamming into the wall. Splitting wood cracked as Flesch fell forward. I watched history repeat itself.

Serras walked over to me. "I caught some of your act. Nice moves."

I looked over at Leo Flesch's still form, back at Serras. "You, too."

We stared at each other.

"I think this is the moment when you crush me to your manly chest and kiss me like I've never been kissed before."

I was right.

Chapter Sixteen

I was sitting on the front step, scanning the Help Wanted section. Paul's house had sold, and the profit was seeing me through until I found gainful employment. Most of the money from Herschmann had been put into a trust for Lucy's children, the rest donated to a nonprofit rehabilitation center for addiction. As Billie had advised, I had invested it wisely. I did take some of the house money and buy some new earrings for Auntie and a full body massage with oils from a blonde named Sven for Adrienne.

I was pondering the pros and cons of the lingerie home party industry when a car pulled into the drive. I looked over the top of the paper and saw Serras in a shiny sport convertible. He slipped his mirrored sunglasses atop his head. His hair was longer, his eyes on me as black as the car's exterior. I set the paper on the step, stood and walked over to him.

"Nice wheels," I told him.

"Hop in. I'll give you a ride."

I shook my head. The other cop with Flesch caught on the video had begun to sing, taking down some of his colleagues and a few of the big boys that could lead to an eventual conviction of Figuero. After a ten-hour surgery, Sam had been saved, and Billie had voluntarily come forward with anything she knew. The indomitable Fiona had recently relocated to Bermuda where I'm sure she was driving the natives wild.

Not long after, Serras had received a package with a palm tree in its postmark and inside a computer disk with names, numbers, trucking logs and payments received. An investigation had begun, was proceeding cautiously. As more evidence came to light, it was becoming increasingly difficult to know who were the bad guys and who were the good. Except for the man that stood before me now.

Still I was not quite ready to take any more rides offered by Alexi Serras.

Serras reached over the seat into the back. "I've got something for you." He set a book bag on the seat beside him. It was unzipped, inside was a textbook, Papermate pens, a notebook. I reached for the notebook. A course syllabus was taped inside its front cover.

I looked up at Serras. "Where did you get these?"

"Out of a trash can."

I thought back. The day I'd thrown these away, I had seen Serras right after. He'd said he'd been pulling into the campus. He must have seen me throw away my book bag and text.

"I figured one day you would want them."

I tipped my head back to contemplate him. "What would make you think that, Serras."

"Because you never sell yourself short." He looked at me, smiled a little and looked incredibly smug. And incredibly sexy. I held his gaze.

"Registration for the last six-week summer session starts today on the campus. Hop in. I'll give you a ride over." His smile broadened a little wider. "I'll even let you drive."

I smiled back, didn't even pretend to hesitate as I reached for the door handle. After all, I thought, as I slid in next to Serras and punched the gas, I now knew better. No one gets away scot-free.

10

When Michael stepped inside the *basso,* the room at street level, he knew that this indeed was Piero's home and not the apartment of some unwitting benefactor whose keys and tuxedo Piero had managed to borrow. More than half the room was taken up with a huge double bed, a *matrimoniale.* It was covered with a clean blue cotton spread, and at the heavy wooden headboard were two oversized plumped-up pillows, suggesting motherly breasts more than hedonistic props. Piero had brought his motorbike in with him, much the way one might in olden days have brought in one's mule or one's horse. To complete the comparison, Piero threw a thick woolen blanket, dark green, over the motorbike, bedding it down for the night.

Against the wall was the kitchen chair Michael had seen the other night, but now it was used to hold a television set. There was another television set on the floor, and still another on one of the four cement steps that seemed to lead to nowhere except into darkness. He considered giving Piero his watch outright, but that would deprive the young man of the opportunity to exercise his skills. The undetected theft was more important to Piero than the profit his cunning might provide. Michael wagered

..imself that Piero would succeed without his knowing and
..ed forward to winning the bet.

"You want more to drink?" Piero reached down into what
would have been his cleavage and brought up the bottle of Cour-
voisier. What for Assunta Spacagna was a repository for medals,
scapulars, and poison was, for Piero, a fair-sized compartment
ready to receive whatever might strike the young man's fancy.
Michael expected him next to dip in and bring out the two glasses,
but apparently the magic act was over. Piero went to the shelf
to the left of the door and took down two glasses, which he held
up to the light, this time not searching for dust but to give Michael
a chance to admire them. They were admirable indeed, delicate
and clear and exquisitely wrought.

"Sit down," Piero said. "Be comfortable. I'll be right back."
He handed Michael the bottle, went up the steps, and disappeared
into the dark. Michael listened for the opening or closing of a
door, but no sound came down, not even footfalls.

Michael had two chairs to choose from—actually three, but
he didn't feel he had the right to dethrone the television set. An
easy chair was angled into a corner, with a floor lamp next to it,
and another kitchen chair was drawn up to a small table to the
right of the street door. The easy chair had the wig on it, the
candelabra poking out. The kitchen chair was empty, but on
the table in front of it was a plate smeared with dried tomato
sauce and a hardening chunk of bread. No fork, spoon, or knife
was visible, but next to the plate was a glass that seemed coated
with milk. Michael couldn't believe Piero drank milk with his
meals, but there it was, the unmistakable gray like a thin syrup
unevenly filming the sides of the glass. There was some left at
the bottom. Michael smelled the glass. He got mostly the scent
of tomato sauce. He pulled the chair away from the table, sat
down, and drank what was left. He held the fluid in his mouth,
testing it, tasting it, like a rare wine, then swallowed. It was milk
and, possibly because of its nearness to the outside wall, deli-
ciously cool.